BEAUTIFUL CRIMINAL

BEAUTIFUL CRIMINAL

GENEVA LEE

ESTATE
PUBLISHING • ENTERTAINMENT

ESTATE PUBLISHING + ENTERTAINMENT

Geneva Lee/Estate Books www.genevalee.com

LATER

I'VE never put much stock in mistakes. Despite the last year of my life, I didn't want my past choices to define me. Now I know I'm doomed to pay for every decision I've made. This is the realization that crashes into me as I fight to stay awake.

Red coats the back of my eyelids as I drift between the real world and the dark. Lights flash, blinding me momentarily as I blink into the rain. It takes a moment for her to come into focus, but when she does everything about her is wrong. Her arms and legs are twisted in unnatural directions like a broken doll. Glass digs into my hands as I claw across the wet pavement toward her. My palm slips as it hits a warm and slippery substance pooling around her head. Her lips are turning blue, but there's a smile fixed on her face as her eyes stare into the starless midnight sky. She looks happy as if she's about to greet a friend. I say her name, I shake her, and then, I scream. And scream. And scream.

"EMMA, you look like hell," my best friend Josie announces to me as I slide into the passenger seat of her beater Civic. I toss my bag onto the floorboard, ignoring the helpful commentary. Instead I pull my wet hair into a messy bun on top of my head. When I don't respond she sighs and reaches into the pile of random junk that she stores in the center console. She tosses a container of concealer at me before she backs out of my driveway.

"This isn't your color," I point out, eyeing the fair shade suspiciously.

"No." She keeps her eyes on the road, but I spot the grin tugging up the corners of her mouth. "It's yours. You're usually the one who needs it."

I raise an eyebrow, which is seriously risky, given that she'll probably deem them in need of intervention.

"Are you sure? Because it seems like you've got a little bitch showing."

"Not my color," she reminds me.

Despite being stuck in standard prep uniform, she looks amazing. Between her corkscrew curls and fuchsia lips, there's an effortless coolness to Josie's style. I guess that's what you get when your mom is a former show girl pretty enough to get knocked up by a high-roller who didn't stick around to place a second bet. Either way he scored big— if only he knew it. Josie has her mom's long legs, ready smile, and way with the men. I say men because she doesn't bother with the guys at school. She prefers to work out her daddy issues with any number of willing tourists.

My dad stands on the porch holding a mug of what I hope is coffee. Josie waves to him cheerfully, narrowly avoiding our mailbox, as I begin to pat the liquid magic on the dark circles rimming my eyes.

"Nightmares? The one about Becca?" She taps the steering wheel, showcasing her fluorescent pink nail polish that looks all that much brighter against her cappuccino skin.

"Test. I had to cram." I lie because I don't want to discuss my seriously screwed up head at seven a.m.

Josie doesn't press it even though she sees through me. She knows the truth because she knows me. That means she also gets that I'm not one to gush about my feelings. What's the point? Talking can't change the shit that's happened.

"Last day," she says instead, "and tonight we party."

"You party," I correct her. "Dad needs me to take over morning shift at the shop first thing on Monday."

"Which gives you a whole weekend, and don't try telling me that you have a hot date."

I flush at the thought. Yeah, hot dates are for girls who haven't been forced into an involuntary vow of celibacy. "I do actually. With laundry and Netflix."

Josie's nose wrinkles and she shakes her head. "You need a life."

"I had one." I stare out the window instantly wishing I hadn't spoken, especially something that made me sound stupid and broken and girly. I'm getting used to the hollow pit my sister's death has left at my core, but today's a day I can't ignore it.

We pull into the school parking lot with my admission hanging like a nasty stink in the air. We both can smell it but we're too polite to talk about it. Josie whips the car so quickly into a space that a nearby frosh jumps out of the way. She shrugs sweetly at him. No one can resist Josie, even if she's just put their life in danger. One of the many reasons that we're an odd couple. I don't smile or chit chat. Hell, I don't make eye contact if I can help it.

"Emma, she wouldn't want you to give up on living," she says in a quiet voice.

"Yeah, well, I wanted to see her graduate this weekend," I snap. She doesn't deserve my reaction, but a year later and I'm still working through the second stage of grief. I prefer when we pretend we're still in denial though.

So much for polite oblivion. I throw my bag over my shoulder, and disappear into the crowd of students scrambling through the front door as the first bell slices the air. This is where I feel safe, lost in a swarm of people who aren't asking if I'm okay or if they can do anything to help. Or worse yet the people who turn those sad eyes on me. I don't want their practiced pity or sympathetic attention. Because there is such a thing as a stupid question and 'are you okay' is one of them. Then there's the jerks that have made it their mission to hold me accountable for what happened that night, because I'm the only one left to blame. The whole lot of them make Belle Mère Prep feel more like the nine circles of hell than high school.

Only a few more hours. But the mental cheer-leading does nothing for my apathy, especially when I spot Hugo Roth, my least favorite mistake, loitering near my English class.

"Hey pawn star, ready for summer vacation?" I don't have to turn to attach the sneer in the voice with his stupid face, but he darts in front of the doorway so I still have to look at him. He's taller than most of the boys in class, which is a blessing given that he has to hold up his gigantic ego all day. I hate to say he cleans up well. Still there's no denying his movie star jawline or his silky blond hair that's just long enough to grab onto when he makes his move. I'd made that mistake once. Never again. "I was thinking of coming into the shop. I have something I know you'll want."

"Sorry. We're all stocked up on junk." My family's Las Vegas pawn shop is considered a tourist landmark, but to me it's just another embarrassment.

I push past him, but his arm flies out to stop me. With his other hand, he grabs his crotch. "What will your daddy give me for this? Or maybe you and I can discuss its value."

"Or maybe I can show it the barrel of one of our many in-stock shotguns." I plaster a smile on my face as I wiggle my pinkie for emphasis. "If I recall, it should slide right in."

Hugo's face darkens as he moves away from the door. "Bitch."

"Good to catch up!" I call after him sweetly from the doorway.

Mr. Hunter doesn't look at me as I rush into the room to the sound of the final bell. "Nice of you to join us, Miss Southerly."

I slide Great Expectations out of my bag and hold it up. "I couldn't stop reading. I didn't get any sleep."

Mr. Hunter has apparently read Dickens because he presses his lips together in disbelief. He probably watched the movie, too, but he doesn't push my tardiness. I slump in my seat as he starts a discussion on whether or not Pip's benefactor did him a favor. Apparently, he didn't get the memo that it's the last day of school. Since I thought the story was stupid—a poor kid trying to impress a rich girl—I stare at the wood-paneling some board member sprung for during the academy's renovation. The result is all Vegas. Oak paneling, bookcases full of dusty leather-bound volumes—a show meant to trick over-qualified teachers and elite college recruiters into thinking that the students here are as competitive as east coast prep students.

Growing up in Belle Mère, I know the truth: all that glitters isn't gold.

"Miss West?" Mr. Hunter calls across the room to a blonde with her back turned to him, catching my attention.

Monroe West glances over her shoulder and stares at him like she's waiting for him to answer. Her Jimmy Choo's probably cost a week of his pay and she knows it. Who said our priorities aren't in place at Belle Mère Prep? But when you're a West, doors open for you. Just not Southerly doors. After Monroe put a pink streak in her hair, Clark County ran out of dye for two months. Girls drove to Los Angeles to get theirs done, and by the time, they had their appointments, she'd moved on. Her latest look is more Miami than pop star, bright citrus hues. She's a step ahead of the game. With her daddy's money and her latest stint on reality TV, wannabe designers are falling all over themselves to send her clothes. It's more proof that life isn't fair. The girl could buy anything she wants and she doesn't even have to. But it's not class warfare that has her on my blacklist. No, she's earned her spot and then some.

"Do you have thoughts on the question?" he prompts her when she doesn't respond.

"Of course, he did him a favor. Everyone wants money. I'd rather be dead than poor." She flicks her bleached locks over her shoulder and returns to her previous conversation.

A snort escapes me and they both turn to stare. Acknowledging Monroe said something is akin to drawing a line in the sand. Generally I stick to cold war tactics like pretending she doesn't exist. It's better for my sanity, but maybe the fact that I won't have to see her for three months is encouraging a little confrontation.

Mr Hunter crosses his arms over his tweed jacket like a nerdy referee. "It seems Emma has some thoughts on the subject."

"Yes." Actual thoughts. "There are so many worse things than being poor like being sick or smug or conceited. I think he knows that. Money doesn't equal happiness." At least, Ethan Hawke didn't seem very happy in the movie, I add silently.

Monroe flips her tan, middle finger at me behind Hunter's back.

"Or class," I add dryly.

She smirks, showcasing how well her coral lipstick matches her manicure. But all evidence of her addition to our debate disappears as soon as Mr. Hunter looks to her. I don't bother to listen as he tries to engage more students in the discussion. It might be Belle Mère policy to educate us until the last possible moment, but we took finals last week. Reading Dickens was the English Department's idea of an end of the year treat. Old Charles would be disappointed to know that we've all checked out, counting the hours until today's final bell heralds the start of summer vacation. Or in my case, summer servitude haggling with gambling addicts over baseball cards and old records. Despite that, this is our version of New Year's Eve as we watch the clock and wait for liberation from one more year.

"If anyone hasn't finished reading, please take your copy with you this summer. The school can afford the loss," Mr. Hunter informs us as the bell rings.

Everyone abandons their unwanted Dickens' novels on their desks as they stampede out of the classroom.

"Emma," Hunter calls before I get to the door. "You're signed up for AP Lit next year, right?"

I nod, chewing on my lip as the hallway fills with students. Contrary to today's tardiness, I hate being late. There's not much I can control in my life but my punctuality.

"I'll send you the reading list over email. I look forward to having you in class again next fall. Take the book with you."

Translation: he's thrilled that the whole class won't be filled with Housers. Kids who are set to inherit casinos and clubs don't have much interest in literature. "Me too."

I dash into the hallway before he can continue the conversation. Hunter is fine but I'll tackle the reading when I visit Mom in Palm Springs next month. Right now, I want to get to class and finish out this day, so I can leave the worst year of my life behind.

THE TEXTS START JUST after lunch. I sneak a few replies but there's nothing I can do while I'm in class. Dad didn't show to the shop, which is a surprise to no one, except his manager Jerry, who is possibly more sheep than man. He needs someone to follow, so without Dad he's lost. By three, Dad is still MIA. I guess it wasn't coffee in his cup this morning. If I'm lucky our next month's mortgage isn't currently riding on number fourteen.

Jerry: Can you come in?

Me: Nope. Plans.

With a half dozen unfinished television seasons.

Jerry: At least, you'll be here on Monday.

And for the rest of my life. Families stick together in Vegas no matter what cards are dealt to them. I'm not stupid enough to believe I'll get out. Here the House always wins and puts you right back in your place.

Another text arrives, this one from mom, apparently I'm expected at brunch in the morning. My one weekend off before the drudgery of a summer job is quickly being taken over by everyone else. I stuff my phone into my bag and allow myself to enjoy exiting Belle Mère Prep. It's a short-lived pleasure, but then again most are. Outside, the parking lot is a sea of convertibles with their tops down. Apparently it was drive mommy's mid-life crisis to school day. Funny, I don't remember that being on the school announcements.

"We are seniors!" Josie shrieks, lunging toward me as soon as I'm down the front steps. I accept the hug because Josie is a hugger and if after seventeen years she hasn't figured out that I'm not, it's a lost cause.

Over her wild mop of hair, a familiar set of brown eyes flickers my way. I pull back in time to spot Jonas take Monroe's hand. Between his lanky form and dark hair and her platinum locks and petite, swimsuit model body, they're a perfect contrast to one another.

Belle Mère's power couple.

Everyone who is anyone wants to be them. Me? I'll admit it. I just want to be her. Maybe since I used to be the one holding his hand.

Josie follows my gaze and her dark eyes narrow when she sees the pair. "Ignore them."

"I am." If only it were as simple as following her command, but Jonas is the one who broke my heart. He kissed me. He made me fall in love. Then he walked away for her, so I jumped into bed with the school's resident narcissist to get back at him.

It would have been nice to know Hugo had placed a bet on how fast he could get me into bed. I'd known I was a sure thing. At least I could have made some money. I didn't get much else out of it.

"I want to go out tonight." I say it before the thought fully processes.

Josie bounces, looking a bit too much like the ex-cheerleader she is, as she rubs her hands together.

"Nothing crazy," I warn her.

"Don't worry. It will be fun, because I know exactly where we're going." The mischievous glint in her eyes sends a wave of apprehension surging through me.

What have I gotten myself into?

2

THE shades are drawn when I reach home. Possibly the only thing more depressing than miles of blazing desert as far as you can see is a dark house smack in the middle of it. The only thing worse than that? The unwelcome scent of stale beer that meets me at the door. I pause for a moment, surveying the scene and wondering why I hadn't signed up for summer classes. I could have graduated early next year, enrolled part time in Las Vegas Community College and used the meager money I made at the shop to get my own place. I allow myself to consider this for all of five seconds before I begin collecting beer cans and cigarettes.

"Hey, pumpkin," Dad greets me, rubbing his eyes. He hasn't passed out yet, which is the only bright spot in this scene. "How was school? Do you have homework?"

My father has been asking those two questions every day of my life since mom left. It's a lack-luster attempt at parenting but I appreciate the effort.

"Last day of school," I remind him, cradling cans in my arms.

"That's right. I got my days mixed up." He scratches his head, smiling sheepishly. "We should celebrate."

Dad tries, which is more than I can say for most parents around here. Most of my classmates were raised by the staff while their parents focused on the casino floor and keeping the whales happy. I wish I could say I was better off than the rest of them, but I'd spent the last five years holding our dysfunctional family together and keeping the business afloat.

He'd never gotten over losing mom, but she'd followed the money away from signed records and sports memorabilia and all the other junk we gave a home to at Pawnography. Apparently a seedy pawn shop blocks from the strip wasn't the kind of wealth she'd envisioned. Mom wanted more and she got it in the form of a new husband and a tasteful compound in Palm Springs where she spent her day sipping white wine spritzers. On her wedding day, she told my sister and I that all her dreams had finally come true. Becca gave her a pass, saying she was simply in love. My sister could see the big picture, including the doors his money would open for us. She'd jumped at the chance to ditch Las Palmas High School when he offered, but

I'd wanted no part of her new life. I finally agreed to attend Belle Mére Prep on her dime only after Josie had gotten a scholarship there. I couldn't stand the idea of starting high school with both my sister and best friend there without me.

I drop the cans in the recycling bin, ignoring the fact that he dumped his ash tray in it. As I open the blinds, the sun hits me and I wonder what mom is doing now. Probably sitting by the pool while someone else cooks her dinner. Or maybe she's already on the private jet heading here to grace me with her presence.

"Where do you want to go? I know a guy over at the Rio who can hook us up at the buffet." Dad rubs his hands over his hair to tame it. He looks like a lot of other men in Vegas at the moment: unshaven and unwashed in yesterday's clothes. Unlike those other men, though, he's handsome with a strong jaw and salt and pepper hair. I've had the displeasure of watching women fall all over him since I was a kid. It's how he landed mom—looks and potential. It turns out looks can't make up for failure.

"Actually, Josie is dragging me out, so you are off the hook." I cringe at the thought of graduation parties. They might be as dangerous as the all-you can eat seafood buffet that he's offering me, but she'd made me swear I wouldn't back out.

"Maybe tomorrow," he suggests.

"Sure." I say noncommittally. That way when he forgets tomorrow I won't be disappointed. It's a survival mechanism I'd adopted since the first time he forgot my birthday.

Grabbing a few things from the fridge I start dinner. There's always food in the house because I take care of that. I shop and I plan. Dad doesn't bother to eat unless I put a meal in front of him, so there's no danger of coming home to an empty fridge. I dump sauce into a pan and start boiling water for pasta. I can't claim it's gourmet given the cheap ingredients, but I can produce spaghetti in under fifteen minutes. Take that Spago.

"This is really good, honey." Dad twists his fork, collecting another bite, and shoves it into his mouth.

"I'll put some in the fridge and you can heat it up for lunch." It's a lost cause. His entire diet consists of coffee, beer, and dinner if I'm around to cook.

He nods. We talk about summer plans and the shop. I have to remind him that I'm going to graduate next year. After I clean up the dishes, I peek into the living room where he's turned on a sporting event. I know this because there is a ball and men trying to beat each other up to get it. My father's obsession with sports did not transfer to me. On the upside that probably means his sports gambling problem won't either.

"I'm going to grab a shower. Let Josie in?"

He raises his beer in acknowledgment of my request.

I stay under the hot water so long that my skin is tight by the time I abandon it. I can't wash away my problems, but I can go out tonight and forget them. Wrapping a towel around my head, I wipe off the mirror with my palm. My cheeks are flushed which is the closest I get to having color. Unlike my peers I don't spend all afternoon worshipping the god of skin cancer. Of course that means I have bluish circles under my eyes and every single blemish sticks out like a sore thumb.

By the time I towel dry my hair and head to my room, Josie is waiting. A few shimmery scraps of cloth are scattered over my bed. I narrow my eyes as I pick one up. No matter how I hold it up, I can't decide what it is.

"Is this a scarf?" I ask finally.

Josie snatches it away. "That's mine thank you very much."

As long as she isn't going to make me wear it, I have no further comment on the issue. She strips down and pulls it on over her thong. It's a skimpy, black romper that dips to her naval.

"I have no boobs," she complains as she tugs at it.

"Look on the bright side," I say as I snag a pair of panties from my drawer, "if you did, you wouldn't be able to wear that."

"I guess you're right." She twists around observing herself in my vanity mirror. "How do I look?"

"Older than you are," I say dryly. It's the answer she wants to hear. Josie's hair is a wild, mop of curls that mesh nicely with her high cheekbones and wide, espresso eyes. Her looks combined with that outfit will get her into any club in town. I'll be riding her coattails or rather g-string to get myself inside. "Where did you find this?"

"Frederick took mom to the desert for the weekend. I borrowed a few things." She pushes a dress into my hands. Josie and her mom are as close as I have to female role models in my life. I'm not exactly preening myself to become a trophy wife like my own mother. So Josie and Marion Deckard are the closest I have to a girl squad. That's definitely how it works between the two of them. Considering Marion is only thirty-five, the two of them act and look more like sisters than mother and daughter.

"This dress is missing the dress." I whip around to check the back of Josie's pre-approved party apparel absolutely certain that my ass is hanging out.

Josie shakes her head, pressing a finger to her mouth like she's deep in thought regarding my ensemble. "Emma, you look hot."

"Perhaps," I say slowly, because part of me digs the glittery, slip of fabric she's talked me into, "but I'm going to have to walk with my thighs smashed together all night." I demonstrate what it looks like to walk with my knees clamped together.

"Stop it!" She tosses a throw pillow from the mound of decorative accents I keeps on my bed. "Make sure you have on cute underwear. Have you waxed lately?"

I scrunch my nose up. "The state of my lady bits aren't up for discussion."

"Your lady bits could use a little discussion," she corrects me.

"They have nothing to gossip about. California isn't the only one with a drought."

A smirk curls Josie's lips. "If you really want to end the dry spell, don't wear anything underneath."

"The old no-panties trick? So 1990s. I thought I'd fake a fainting spell instead." There were easier ways to advertise a vacancy than putting it on display. Besides in Vegas what's one more vagina crying out for attention? "So what trouble are you getting us into?"

"Nope." She shakes her head as she holds out a tube of lipstick. "It's a surprise."

I groan and press my hands together. "Please. I beg you."

She only smiles. Whatever she has planned can't be good if she has to drag me there. "Do I get a blindfold?"

"The party isn't that kinky," she says with a snort.

"So it's a party!"

"No shit, Sherlock." She rolls her eyes as she fluffs my hair. It's a lost cause. We are the yin and yang of hair— her unruly, sexy curls and my stick-straight honey blonde locks.

"Why won't you tell me?" I ask her as she continues to make me up.

"That's why you're going easy on me," she says.

"Allowing me to put mascara on you isn't going to get me to spill. I'm not that easy."

I stick my tongue out and immediately regret the move when she smacks it with a make-up brush. "That's not what I heard."

"That all you got, Southerly?" She plants one hand on her hip and instantly looks just like her mother. I don't mention this lest I get smacked with another make-up brush. "Because you need to bring it tonight."

That's exactly what I was afraid she would say.

3

IT'S a bad sign when Josie wants to Uber. That means two things: she's getting drunk and we're headed to the Strip. It's weird being a duo when we used to be a trio. Becca and Josie used to outnumber me all the time. Now that Becca's gone, we're more evenly matched. Josie still wins most times. I guess she's luckier than I am.

I once tried to see the heart of Las Vegas through the eyes of a stranger—the lights, the people, a million glittering attempts to grab your attention. But I couldn't. Now all I can see is the reality. Behind the crowds of tourists and the Bellagio fountains, under the designer shopping and a-list shows, everyone is broken. It's the ultimate twist of the American dream: pull a lever and you might have it all. Ride out another roll of the dice and you'll become someone. Vegas was built on destroying people. It still is. I wish knowing that could save me, but you don't get out of a town like this. Maybe my luck will change, but I'm not holding my breath.

Our driver flies in and out of traffic so quickly that the neon becomes streaks of color outside the window.

"So what's tonight? Japanese businessmen or the no limits room?" I ask still looking out the glass. We don't gamble, but I know exactly where she prefers to drift when she heads out.

"Neither. Tonight we are young," she announces. "Besides I can always call Richard later."

"The oil guy?"

"No, he's in finance."

"You need a therapist." I abandon the view and turn to her. I've only told her this about a million times.

"Only if he's hot."

I groan. "And old. Where are we going?"

Josie bites her lip and my whole body tenses. A surprise is one thing, but she can't hide the guilt on her face.

"Are you shanghaiing me?" I demand, grabbing for her phone. She holds it away and I resort to tickling her, nervous peels of laughter squeaking from her. But before I can elicit a confession, the car slows down. I stare at the doors to the resort.

"Are you fucking kidding me?" I ask as a bell boy opens the door. I don't wait for her to respond, instead I walk the opposite direction back toward the street. There's no way I'm going into the West.

Josie catches me by the arm before I make it past the entrance, but I don't stop. We're both in impractically tall heels, which means one of us is going down. Spoiler: it won't be me.

"Em," she pleads, "just hear me out."

But there's no point to listening. "I thought you understood the social food chain, but let me make it easy. We're on bottom. If my dad finds out I'm here he'll disown me."

"It's the end of the year party. Everyone will be there!"

"Everyone who was invited," I correct her. My name will never be on a West guest list and I'm one hundred percent okay with that, considering that the price of admission is your soul.

Josie produces a small card from her purse and flourishes it inches from my face. "We're invited."

"Where did you get that?" My anger ebbs into annoyance. That invite is probably enough to get us past security but that's only the first test. The rest of the gauntlet is composed of Monroe and her bitchy minions.

"It doesn't matter. This party is going to be packed."

In Josie speak that means everyone is going to be there, including all the people she'd like to impress.

"You do realize that even with that"—I point to the invitation—"we're not welcome up there."

That finally extinguishes the hopeful glimmer in her eyes. I can't call it a victory because now she just looks pissed. Josie crosses her arms, still clutching the invite, and glares at me. "Since when do you care what people think?"

"I don't."

"Then why not crash, drink their booze, and ruin their nights."

"Well-played." Josie has a point. I can't help but picture Monroe West's face when she discovers the breach in her castle walls. It will be even better to see her horror in person. "Fine, but we stick together and we don't stay long. I have to make a cameo at brunch tomorrow to appease the maternal monster."

I can think of about a million things I'd rather do than spend the evening with a bunch of Housers, including washing my hair, getting a pap smear, and tearing off my own fingernails. Girls just wanna have fun, right?

Meanwhile Josie is positively vibrating with excitement. I let her take my hand and lead me to the entrance of the casino where we're greeted by another uniformed lackey. If only he knew he was letting a Southerly walk inside the West empire. Yeah, we might have just cost him his job, but it's not my responsibility to provide a PSA to the newbie.

Emma Southerly, daughter of Jake Southerly, the

mortal enemy of Nathaniel West, owner of the West Resort and Casino.

It sounds melodramatic but it's true. The feud between my dad and Monroe's father goes back from before I was born. They'd been high school buddies. In college they scrounged up every penny they had between the two of them to invest in a start-up. When the start-up took-off, my dad assumed they'd both made it big until he found out Nathaniel had invested it in his name only. Nathaniel West became a venture capitalist super-star and left my dad to take over the family pawn shop. My father had instilled hatred of the type usually reserved for rival sports teams in me my whole life. Since I've never met Nathaniel, I do my part by loathing his daughter. Every one has a role to play after all. Plus Monroe is easy to hate.

Inside the revolving door, the cacophony of the casino floor greets me immediately. Cigarette smoke, dealers calling for bets, hundreds of melodic slot machines. It's enough to make me want to turn tail and abandon Josie but she marches us through the crowds toward the bank of sleek elevators on the other side before I can process any of it. But let's face it, there is no processing it. It's a world of distraction meant to keep you so overwhelmed that you don't notice your savings account is slipping away. The lights, the noise —it's guerrilla warfare at its finest.

Josie walks directly to the elevator at the end and

the bag of muscles stationed in front of it. "I'm a guest of Monroe West."

I refrain from gagging at that proclamation.

The private elevator only goes to one floor: the top. Despite that being the seventy-fifth floor, the car travels like lightning, giving me no time to steel myself before the doors slide open to deposit us in a massive entry hall. Because the gold elevator wasn't extravagant enough the entirety of the foyer—floor to ceilings is polished, black marble.

"It's not too late to leave," I point out as the sounds of the party begin to seep toward us.

"Take the chicken exit?" Josie arches her eyebrow.

"Fine, lead the way." My gaze travels up the wall and I catch sight of myself. It doesn't look like me thanks to Josie's wardrobe choices. The girl trapped in the marble is older, put together, sexy. Maybe it's what I hope to be someday. Most days I'm lucky to have all the pieces to my prep uniform clean.

"You cool?" Josie prompts and I realize I've stopped in my tracks.

I tug at the hem of my dress and shrug. "I was just wondering if Nathaniel West read The Great Gatsby too many times, because truly he's compensating for something."

"Not for his money," Josie giggles.

The elevator door dings and I realize that in the time it's taken me to get a hold of myself it's traveled back to the lobby and up again.

"Let's go," I urge her. There's no telling who will be inside. We stand a much better chance of not getting kicked out if we don't come face to face with one of Monroe's minions. I was a Girl Scout. I know there's safety in numbers.

But before we can reach the hallway, footsteps fall behind us. Instinctively, I look over my shoulder and catch sight of Nathaniel West. He's the same age as my dad but he's obviously spent some money on looking younger. That or maybe stress and bitterness are prematurely aging my father. He studies us, a slight sneer creeping onto his lips. There's no denying he's good-looking, exactly the kind of guy Josie throws herself at. Square jawed and broad-shouldered with salt and pepper hair and an expensive suit. But the look he gives me chills my blood, freezing me to the spot. He's a predator and he has me in his sights. One move and I'll be at his mercy. I want to run or hide. Instead I can only shrink back still locked in place and hope his interest in me fades.

Because more than the casual interest he's showing me, there's something in his blue eyes that flickers darkly. It's what holds me in place: this terrifying magnetizing force. Does he know who I am? Would he even care? If Monroe West walked into the pawn shop I doubt my father would blink. He'd probably get a sick thrill out of buying whatever she offered, because it meant a West was in his territory. No doubt that Nathaniel would feel the same way knowing the Jacob Southerly's daughter had found herself in his home.

The men say nothing to us as they pass. Josie tugs at my elbow, urging me forward but before we can follow Nathaniel into the house, one of his bodyguards steps in front of us. He extends his finger, pointing to the opposite hallway.

"The party is that way. This wing is closed to Miss West's guests."

He's firm but not unkind as he speaks. I bite my lip and nod. It takes more than a fair amount of authority to shut me up. This guy has it in spades.

As soon as we're out of earshot, I fall against a wall. "If Dad knew I was that close to Nathaniel West, he'd kill one of us."

Josie nods, still struck dumb by the chance encounter.

I have to admit that after that a swarm of Housers is a welcome sight. The party is already in full swing and in typical Vegas fashion, there's a train wreck everywhere we turn. It's obvious we're not the only ones who crashed or maybe Hugo invited all his favorite escorts. Judging from the scantily clad girls lounging around him, that might be the case. I guide Josie to the outskirts of the room wanting to avoid him.

"Let's get a drink!" I suggest. Maybe it will help wash the taste of self-loathing from my mouth.

Josie only nods.

"Hey, you okay?" I call over the crowd.

She nods again. That's a no. Josie has always craved the attention of the Housers, something I can't exactly fault her for. She's had a lot less time getting kicked around by them. I, on the other hand, floated between the worlds. My dad's business wasn't exactly brag-worthy, but since all commerce in sin city operated in various shades of vice, that might have been a moot point. His rivalry with Nathaniel was what had destroyed any chance I had at belonging. My mother's remarriage to a successful movie producer had nearly wiped that slate clean. When I started Belle Mère, I'd been given a shot at being part of the elite. Monroe, herself, wanted to French braid my hair. Until I started dating Jonas. When she stole him away, I lost my boyfriend and the few friends I thought I had outside of Josie and Becca. The accident just put the final nail in my reputation with the Housers and reduced my inner circle by one.

Josie's never had a cent to her name, though. Knowing me was as close as she came to the in-crowd. She's never had any way to draw attention.

However, she snagged that all-access pass, this is her chance to make a name for herself. I want to warn her against it, but how do you tell your best friend that her fantasy is actually a nightmare in the making.

You don't. That's why I came inside. Because if this is what Josie wants, I'll be beside her.

That also means I'll be there to pick up the pieces.

Until then booze is definitely in order. I drag her through the living room to the bar.

"What will you have?" a kid playing bartender calls over the crowd.

"Two shots of whiskey." I hold up my fingers for emphasis. He dribbles on the counter as he pours. He's going to need a replacement soon. Knowing Monroe, she'll call someone up from the casino to perform the honors. I hand one to Josie and we down them swiftly.

"Better?" I ask when she's recovered from the liquid courage.

"Yes!" She wiggles away from the bar, her mood shifting instantly.

We weave through the crowd, a few lightweights are already on the floor. I step over a girl, biting my lip, torn over leaving her there. But when I move closer, I don't see the girl, I see my sister. Stumbling back, the girl's friend pushes past me. She shoots me a disgusted look.

"I can't believe you would just leave her like that."

I mutter an apology before whipping around to look for a way outside. Anxiety is a bitch and she's always crashing the party. By the time I find one I'm sucking desperately for air.

You didn't leave her, I remind myself. You didn't leave her.

I didn't leave her, and it didn't matter.

It takes a second to catch my breath and then I remember where I am. The rooftop patio contains a collection of cabanas and, even in the dark, it's obvious they're occupied. I look away, feeling like a perv only to discover a pool full of my naked classmates. The pool itself extends to the edge of the building. It probably offers a pretty amazing view but right now, the number of boobs on display has temporarily blinded me. This clearly isn't the sanctuary I'm seeking.

Josie didn't follow me outside, which means I've lost her to the crowd. I wait a few minutes, hoping she'll find her way out to me. Despite the HBO level of nudity in progress, it's still safer here than in there. I count to one hundred before I give up and head into the fray.

"My favorite conquest!"

I force a smile as Hugo greets me at the door with his harem. He's wearing a shirt that proudly proclaims 'STD free.'

"That's false advertising," I inform him, planting my hands on my hips.

"You're welcome to check." He grins widely, tossing his arms around the girls closest to him.

"You really should pay them more. They can't even afford clothes," I say dryly.

The blonde on his left's mouth falls open but the redhead on his right just looks bored.

"Jealousy isn't becoming, Emma." He emphasizes each syllable, the sound of my name on his lips plucks at me.

I've been ID'ed by Hugo, which means it's time to find Josie and get home. I only get a few steps from him before Monroe lunges at me. Her fingers dig into my arm, and I have to resist the urge to slap her. She studies me with disgust. Apparently the scrap of cloth I'm wearing isn't as designer as the scrap of cloth she's wearing. This close I realize she has the same blue eyes as her father. But whereas his blazed, hers are as cold as ice.

"You're going to break a nail," I warn her.

"Who let you up here?"

"Nice guy down stairs. Little head, big muscles. Wait, I'm not sure that narrows it down. How many cavemen do you employ here anyway?" I yank away from her.

Her closest friends flank her, each girl dressed in a slightly different shade of pink. Leighton is blush, and Sabine is bashful. Apparently they've not been given the thumbs up to adopt Monroe's grapefruit hue. Monroe, Leighton and Sabine —the three of them are a veritable spectrum of evil. Leighton is a state-dependent bitch. Get her alone and she's actually not a terrible human being, but either Monroe flips a switch in her or she's far too eager to impress the Housers. Monroe is Monroe. Sabine, on the other hand? Click on crazy bitch in Urban Dictionary and you'll find her picture. Most of the rumors aren't true. Like the one about her pushing some freshman off the roof of the gym? I sincerely doubt even her parents could cover that up. The rub is that she is totally capable of pushing someone off a roof.

I guess there's a little bit of truth in everything.

"Leighton. Sabine." I nod in greeting. "I had no idea they were filming a Pepto Bismal ad tonight. Congrats on the gig."

"You need to leave." It's amazing Monroe actually produces sound given how tightly she's gritting her teeth.

"Is that anyway to treat a guest?" Riling her up is a calculated risk but I need to buy time before security escorts me off the premises. But even as I scan the crowd around her, I can't find Josie. Over half of Belle Mère but no best friend. I check my phone again, but there's no response to my S.O.S.

Monroe whispers furiously to Leighton. No doubt placing a takeout order. It would be so like her to not even kick me out herself. In the periphery, Jonas moves into view, his gaze flicking from me to Monroe and back again. It's been a long time since I felt those eyes on me, and I hate how it twists my stomach into knots.

Coming here was a mistake.

"Don't bother," I interrupt. "I'm going."

I don't bother trying to look graceful as I push my way through the crowd, but I keep my head up. Jonas and I have had a good thing going, each of us pretending the other doesn't exist. If that unspoken treaty is no longer in effect than I plan to stay as far away from him and Monroe and here as possible. I guess it's a good sign that seeing him no longer makes me want to cry. I think that's what they call progress.

Before I can make it back to the elevators, Jonas intercepts me at the door. His eyes are warm like melted chocolate as he stops. I used to love staring into those eyes. Now I can barely stand to eat a Hershey's bar. That's love for you: the destroyer of life's simple joys.

"Look Monroe is all bark and no bite," he promises, shoving his hands into his pockets. It's a classic Jonas move. He can't stand to have anyone feel left out. If Monroe is the poster child for bitchy behavior, he's the peacemaker. Yet another reason I've deemed their union unholy. Now he's standing here, talking to me, as if I'm just one of the other kids' she's always bullying.

I cross my arms over my chest. He might be able to justify her attitude but there's no way I'm willing to play along. "Then put her on a leash."

"She's just very particular about her guest list. I'm sure if you—"

"We both know why she doesn't want me here," I interrupt him, "but don't worry whatever fit of insanity I suffered earlier is over. I'm leaving."

"You don't have to go." I hate how his voice softens around those words. We stare at each other, and I wonder if this is just him doing his good samaritan act or if he actually wants me to stay. Butterflies stir in my stomach and I squash the fragile hope before I do or say something stupid. I push past him. "I need to find Josie."

He forces a wounded smile, but let's me leave. When I reach the foyer, I still haven't found Josie. She isn't responding to texts. The security guard who pointed us in the direction of the party is gone. It occurs to me then that I'm as lost to her as she is to me.

"You were going to get kicked out anyway," I say to the empty hall before I take a deep breath and follow in the footsteps of Nathaniel. If I'm lucky I'll find her first, but let's face it, lady luck is a bitch.

4

THE West residence goes on forever. There's wealth and then there's extravagance but this rises to the highest levels of selfishness. The other half of the home has been crowded with warm bodies making it too difficult to see my posh surroundings. The marble floor continues down the hallway, satiny gold papers the wall. I trail my hand along it. The slight texture of the wallpaper vibrates across my fingertips. Overhead a series of miniature chandeliers lights my way, dripping like luxury icicles. Who said Vegas was gauche? Sometimes I wonder if this is where interior design flunkies get sent.

I don't mean to count the rooms as I pass them but after the fifth bathroom I'm shaking my head. They can't possibly use them all. Maybe they have a rotation going or they use one for each day of the week. Monday's bathroom. Tuesday's bathroom. Wednesday's bathroom. The maid service should be given the Medal of Honor.

Light creeps through the crack of the slightly ajar door. I pause outside and consider my options. I can keep creeping around counting bathrooms or I can gamble. Pressing my palm to the door, I realize I have a little Vegas in me after all. It swings open to reveal an empty room. A large glass desk perched on chrome legs sits in front of the floor-to-ceiling windows that overlook the neon lights of the strip. A pair of high-back leather chairs in glossy black wait in front of it. It's an office but other than a crystal decanter filled with amber liquid and two rocks glasses, it's devoid of personality. No books. No papers. No art hanging on the walls. Then again what could compete with the glittering backdrop of sin city?

"I don't think you're supposed to be in here."

I startle at the sound of the disembodied voice, my hand flying to my chest like a bad actress.

"S-s-sorry," I stammer as I begin to back out of the room. I've been caught sneaking around by Nathaniel West. I guess I'll finally find out if casino owners really have the power to break someone's legs or if that's just an urban legend.

The desk chair spins around slowly revealing the owner of the voice. As he comes into the light I know he's wearing jeans instead of a suit and that the thin T-shirt hugs his biceps. He clutches the arms of the chair with broad strong hands that bear no signs of age. By the time the light hits his face I know I haven't stumbled upon Nathaniel.

"I don't think you are either, but I won't..." My words die on my lips as his brutally beautiful face is revealed. I've never been the girl who hung pictures of rock stars or actors on my walls. I don't gush over how hot Hottie McHottie is, and I don't turn into a blubbery puddle when I meet a cute guy.

But this guy isn't cute. He isn't hot. He exists on some other plane of attractiveness altogether. His jawline is sharp, chiseled and sculpted by genetics far superior to the rest of humanity. There's a slight crook to his nose that is somehow so perfectly imperfect. A slight smirk plays at his lips. My gaze lingers there wondering what it would be like to kiss him. So much for being above all that boy crazy shit. I'd hang his poster over my bed shamelessly. His tousled brown hair is long enough that I can imagine grabbing it. It's his eyes, though, that arrest me. In the dim light of the room they're deep gray, flashing with dangerous interest. The other half of his face remains in shadow as if I'm only seeing as much of him as he'll allow me to see.

"You're correct." He leans forward pressing his hands flatly against the glass desktop. He's completely in the light now, showcasing the wide curve of his mouth. His eyes are bluer now, the color of the sea after a storm. I could drown in those eyes.

Warning bells ring in my head but my subconscious hits the snooze button. "I won't tell if you won't tell."

"That sounds like a proposition." His eyes trail over my face and my cheeks begin to heat under his watchful gaze.

Two minutes alone with this guy and I've shut down all my defenses. That's the last thing I can allow to happen. "It's not. It's merely playing it smart."

I fold my arms over my chest and tear my eyes from his. He can't be oblivious to his effect on girls, which is why I won't give him the satisfaction of toying with me.

"I didn't mean to offend, Duchess." He shifts in the chair crossing his arms behind his head and no longer bothering to hide his cocky grin.

"You didn't." I study the top of the replica Eiffel tower a few blocks away.

"Then I didn't mean to annoy." He sounds amused but I refuse to check to see if his smile has widened.

"Do I look annoyed?" I shrug and pivot on my heels toward the door. It's well past time for me to take my exit. If Josie is in trouble she'll call. She always does, but not before making me worry a bit. This time though, I'm out. Getting caught trespassing twice in one night is my quota.

He stays silent as I walk toward the door but before I reach the hall, he calls out, "You do look ruffled."

"Ruffled?" I repeat, twirling around to glare at him. "Ruffles are for dresses and potato chips. I don't ruffle."

"Oh, you are definitely ruffled." He brushes a hand

over his hair, somehow managing to make it even messier—and sexier. Natural, coppery highlights glint from it as he laughs.

I plant my hands on my hips. When I find Josie, I'm going to kill her. For now, I'd settle for strangling him. "I'm just not interested in playing games."

"Most girls love games," he says.

"I'm not most girls."

"Of course," he continues without acknowledging that I've spoken, "most girls aren't very good at playing."

"Is that so?" I ask. The flush I feel now has nothing to do with embarrassment.

"They never seem to win." He stands and circles the desk, walking toward me with a swagger that sets off my bad boy alarm.

"Try me."

His eyebrow arches up. I've got his attention now. "How did you get in here?"

"I walked," I answer with a shrug. "This is a terrible game."

"I'm just setting the stage, Duchess."

I groan, dropping my arms to my sides as my hands ball into fists. "That's the second time you've called me that. Why?"

"I'm the one asking questions." He takes a step closer and now I can smell his cologne–leather and spice and sex.

"You asked your question. I asked mine. Quid pro quo."

"Fancy words. I'm going to guess you don't go to Las Palmas." A smile twitches at his lips, making him look both kissable and smackable at the same time.

I bat my eyelashes a bit too fast as I answer. "Who says I go to school?"

Hottie McHottie is turning me into a giggling school girl faster than a cheerleader drops her panties on prom night. I step backward instinctively and bump against the door. So much for a graceful exit. My blunder gives him the opportunity to lean over me. He grips the wood frame, hovering dangerously close. I can't help but get the sense that I'm being stalked. Any moment now he might lunge and devour me.

"The uneducated generally don't drop Latin idioms, even common ones." His words dance over my face, leaving a breathy trail of whiskey. "But I'm impressed, so I'll answer your question on the condition that you answer my early one."

I open my mouth to protest but instead I find myself nodding, hypnotized by the magnetic hold of his gaze. Whoever he is, he has more than a few tricks up his sleeve. I know because I'm already under his spell.

His head slants to whisper in my ear. "You look like a Duchess. Regal. Haughty. Untouchable."

I tuck that description away. Later I'll dissect it, fulfilling the biological imperative of femininity. I suspect I'll be annoyed. Maybe even pissed. For now, though, all I can think is that I don't want to be untouchable, not with his lips so close to my skin.

"Your turn," he prompts, pulling away.

I swallow hard, immediately relieved to have a little more space between us. "I was looking for a friend. I guess I got lost."

"The party is in the other room." He backs away, completely liberating me from the cage of his arms.

"No shit." I stand up straighter. If the predator is going to give his prey a chance to escape, I need to be alert. "It's not really my scene. I wanted to find her to say goodbye."

"I was told this is the party of the year," he says, "but you're here against your will."

"Not against my will. More like against my moral code. Hanging out with Monroe West and her minions has to be a violation of the Geneva Convention."

"Minions?" he says with a laugh. "Is that what you call them?"

"Them? Don't you mean us?" I repeat, tilting my head to size him up. He definitely looks like he belongs in her world. He's too pretty for the eyes of mere mortals and his clothes scream upper one percent.

"So I'm classified as a minion? For what do I owe the honor?"

I reach out and run a finger along the neckline of his thin t-shirt. "Gucci," I guess. "And why not? Who doesn't want to drop a couple Benjamins to look like he's not trying? There's no cheap alcohol lingering in your cologne or on your breath."

"So my taste earns me the coveted title?"

"Minion isn't a compliment," I say flatly. He might want to be playful but I'm not in the mood. "Of course, I don't think you go to Belle Mère and Las Palmas kids don't shop Caesar's." I don't bother to add that I don't either. If the forum shops weren't filled with miles of the most expensive retailers in the world, I'd probably still want to avoid the cheesy Americanization of the ancient world. Although it's debatable if Caesar would be with me on that. No, it was a milestone for nouveau riche tourists, but merely a mall to most of my classmates where Spago is the foodcourt.

"Maybe I stole this. You did catch me where I wasn't supposed to be, remember?" His tongue flicks across his full, lower lip. "What would you say then?"

"Did you?" I breathe. "Grand larceny isn't really a turn-on."

He winks before nodding toward the door. "Well, I'm not a student at Belle Mère or Las Palmas."

Does the help here have sticky fingers? That seems doubtful, especially given the confidence that oozes from him. He was probably a boyfriend from out of town who slipped away from arm candy duty. It would definitely explain his entitled attitude. I watch as he slips out the door, heading back to the party or seeking more treasure to loot. It's hard to decide which way I hope he's heading—back to the Housers or to play Robin Hood.

Away from his presence, I remember where I am. Hanging out in Nathaniel West's study is a surefire way to get an up-close and personal look at the West's security. Still someone should appreciate this view. I linger for a few minutes and drink it in. My impression of the man my father hates so vehemently feels justified standing here. Does he look out over the valley below and see the rest of us bustling about like worker ants building his kingdom? No computer. No pictures. There doesn't seem to be much else to do here but play god. That was the difference between a man like West and my dad. One bled and the other doesn't.

Pivoting on my heels, I stride out of the office. But before I can act on my instinct to get out of here, with or without Josie, a shadowy figure on the stairs catches my eye. I freeze in place, realizing with dread that it's no longer moving either.

Busted.

5

THIS isn't one of those moments when your life flashes before your eyes. Nope, a vision of the next twenty-four hours in a jail cell, waiting for my dad to wake up from a bender, does instead. With any luck Monroe or Hugo will get a couple of great shots of the security hauling me off. By morning, news of my poor judgment will have spread like a pandemic through most of Belle Mère. Oh well. My Instagram feed could use the boost. But when I get the courage to peel my eyes off the floor, I discover the shadow is attached to my new best friend.

"Are you following me?" he asks.

"N-n-no," I stumble over my denial. What is it about this guy that has me tongue-tied? Whatever it is I can't say that I like it. I plant a hand on my hip in challenge. "Are you following me?"

This earns me a smile. The kind that drops

defenses and charms parents. I thought I'd built an immunity to guys like him, but here I am coming down with a bad case of wet panties.

He extends his hand and looks at me expectantly. I shake my head. My judgment isn't completely shot.

"I don't bite."

That's disappointing.

"You suck at introductions. I don't even know your name," I point out.

"Is that all that's stopping you?"

That and a few shreds of common sense that he hasn't obliterated yet. What if he tells me his name? Will I take his hand? What if he doesn't? I'm just as likely to follow him, which means I'm in big trouble. Damn Josie for disappearing on me. Usually I'm the one bailing her out of jams. Tonight I wish she'd return the favor. When I find her, I'm revoking her BFF card.

"It must be something terrible," I tease. "Maybe Howard? Or Bert?"

"Bert?" he repeats with a deep laugh. "Two can play this game you know."

I barely process that we've begun walking deeper into the penthouse. Score one for my self preservation skills.

"Ingrid?" he guesses. "Helga?"

"What am I? An old German woman?"

He pauses unexpectedly and I run directly into him. His hands grip my upper arms, steadying me before I can stumble. His touch does strange things to my body – stuff usually reserved for romance novels.

"Definitely not." His answers scrapes up his throat. Maybe I'm not the only one affected by skin to skin contact. "Jameson. My family calls me Jamie.."

Jamie. That feels far too normal a name for him. Familiar. Comfortable. It doesn't fit how he makes me feel. But Jameson does.

"Your turn," he prompts.

"Oh, is that how this works, Jameson? I thought we were playing coy." At least I can pretend like I have some dignity left.

"We can keep playing, Duchess, but I'm beginning to feel like my opponent deserves formal recognition." The arrogance that's marked his tone since we met softens a bit as he speaks.

"I like the name you've given me. You're right. It's fitting."

His mouth twists into a smirk that's at odds with his strong jaw line, making him look devilish. Why are the wicked boys so much more beddable?

"Duchess it is."

I've won this round and we both know it. It's an unforeseen victory, but I'll take it anyway. I take the opportunity to be the one that leads. A few steps deeper into the penthouse and we find ourselves in a kitchen. Being here has me out of sorts. Scattered mail and magazines clutter the black granite countertops. Judging from the oversized Viking range and large steam hood this is a gourmet kitchen, but the only evidence of food consumption is the dry bits of toast on the plates piled in the sink and an empty yogurt cup.

"I guess the maid has the day off," I note, instinctively picking up the trash and looking for the wastebasket.

"Are you applying for the job?" Jameson asks, nodding toward the offending yogurt cup.

"Maybe for chef." I stare longingly at the stove. I can only imagine the ingredients in the subzero fridge. I bet it's not full of chicken breasts and a half dozen cheap marinades—unlike my house. These people can have whatever they want and they settle for toast and yogurt. Swallowing hard I turn away from the gourmet appliances and spot a neatly disguised recycling bin. It's fitting really: trim out your trash with white-washed paneling so no one knows that you have any. Who would want the ugliness of the used and discarded blemishing their perfect reality? Not the Wests.

"Chef?" He sounds impressed. It's completely gross that his approval sends a tingle running from my scalp to my toes. I ignore how that ripple hesitates a little too long between my legs.

I shrug, doing my best to look nonchalant. I'm pretty certain that's what Cosmo recommends in these situations, pretend like you're too chill to notice the guy is flirting with you. Except I don't know if Jameson is flirting with me. My boy skills need a tuneup. "I like to cook. It's sad the wicked bitch of the West wastes her caloric intake on nonfat Greek yogurt."

"It's a good source of protein," Jameson advises me as he grabs a stool and makes himself at home in the West's kitchen. "Wicked bitch of the West?"

I cringe inwardly. For all I know Jameson is Monroe's childhood buddy. Or more likely, judging from the pythons of biceps peeking from his T-shirt, her bodyguard. "That's what everyone calls Monroe West. I have no idea who came up with it. I can't believe I said that."

Two truths and a lie.

Wicked bitch of the West. I coined that particular term of endearment for Monroe in ninth grade not long after our introduction when she was released from captivity, or boarding school as the Housers call it.

"I take it you're not a fan."

"I wouldn't say that," I hedge. "I mean I watched her on Pop Princess like the rest of school." Monroe's brief foray into reality television had been the talk of Belle Mère, and it had given me a reason to heckle my screen for a couple weeks. I keep that to myself.

"Then not a friend," he clarifies. Those stormy eyes pierce through me. It's not a question. It's clear he knows the answer, but I can't resist responding.

"We aren't planning any slumber parties. You?"

I'm dying for him to tell me how he wound up here. Maybe that's why I've been answering his questions. Of course, it could just be that he's rattling me. If

I'm not careful I'll need to make a cold shower my next stop on this unofficial tour of the West estate.

"I wouldn't call her a friend." It's not much information but judging from the chilly undercurrent in his words he's not the president of her fan club.

Good enough for me.

"Cook something," he says out of nowhere. I shake my head. It's fairly hard to render me speechless but Jameson's just accomplished it.

He snorts at my horrified reaction. "You said it yourself. Someone should appreciate this kitchen. Besides I'm sure one of the—what did you call them? Minions?—will wreck it before the night's over."

He slides off the stool and breaches the subzero fridge, revealing a drawer of artisan cheeses, tins of caviar, and shelves full of perfect organic produce. I have $50 in grocery money to hold me until the end of the month and they have half a Whole Foods in this kitchen.

"Inspired?" He steps aside, holding open the door for me.

"I shouldn't." But now I'm merely feigning a conscience. By this time most of the partygoers will be far too wasted to remember their own names let alone mine. If we get caught I can play drunk. I can't resist the temptation as I pluck a wedge of Gouda from the drawer along with the glass pint of milk. No plastic gallons in this kitchen. Jameson leans against the counter, gripping the edge, as he watches me rummaging through the pantry and fridge for the rest of the ingredients I need. One I've collected the necessities, I fill a Le Creuset stockpot with the special water tap conveniently built into the backsplash over the eight burner gas range. I guess it would have been too much work to use the sink and carry all the way over. "I hope you're hungry."

"I'm starving." His voice is low and gravelly. My eyes flash to his in time to see his tongue flick over his perfectly white teeth.

The better to eat you with.

"Can I help you?" he asks.

"Do you cook?" I don't bother to hide my incredulity at his offer. I can't help but imagine that he subsists on the sandwiches his conquests deliver to him in bed.

"No," he admits slowly and for a moment his cocky exterior slips allowing me a flash of sheepish Jameson. Dammit it makes him even hotter. "But I can set a mean table. Shall we dine poolside?"

He gestures to the private patio just outside a row of sliding glass doors.

"That would be lovely," I practically sing out and he smiles. I can't help my cheerful mood swing now that he's found my soft spot. Not an easy feat. But I've always felt at home in a kitchen. My sister and I used to help our mom cook. She taught me all the basic French sauces. It came in handy when she ditched the three of us for personal chef of her own. I'd split duties with Becca after that. Then everything changed. It had been a long time since I found myself humming over roux.

A few minutes later and I have a slowly thickening cheese sauce and boiling water. Reaching for the bag of penne I found in the cupboard, I dump it in and stir. The pasta momentarily disturbs the waters heat and the surface calms before steam rises to shatter it again. I stare at the bubbles, wondering if I find myself in hot water soon as well.

Jameson returns to the kitchen and I resolve not to look at him. The smell of melted Gouda is drool worthy enough. He passes behind me, opening a drawer, but then his hands are on my hips. My eyes close for a split second, relishing the confident gesture. In that moment I imagine this is my life: cooking without a care in the world for my hot boyfriend. It's so simple that it almost seems attainable.

But it isn't. I gulp against the treacherous ache in my throat. It's a fantasy, that's all. Dreams like that are the lies sold to little kids, and I haven't purchased any for a long time.

He peers over my shoulder, tucking his chin against my neck. It fits there. Maybe a bit too well. "What are you making, Duchess?"

"Grown up mac & cheese," I whisper, not trusting my voice to hide my emotions.

"I might have to see your ID before you can have

that." He sweeps his lips swiftly over my throat before he steps away.

I'm in trouble with a capital T. Or maybe I'm just finally having a good dream for once.

"Nice try. But I know what you're really after. Isn't it more fun if you don't know who I am?" I tap the whisk against the rim of the saucier before I take it off the heat. Then I point to the pot of pasta. "Drain that."

"As you wish."

"I love that movie," I say absently.

Jameson pauses at my side, potholders in hand. "It's one of my favorites."

His arm brushes mine as he reaches for the pot. My insides twist as I watch him dump the water. Neither of us speak as he returns the pot to the stove. I add the sauce, not daring to break the silence. We've fallen under a magic spell. Reality will fuck it up soon enough.

AN HOUR later I'm strewn across a chaise in the pool cabana as Jameson finishes the last of the pasta. I eye him with interest from my carb-induced coma. "Does anyone feed you?"

"Not stuff like this," he says, scooping another bite into his mouth before he pushes the bowl away. "If I could I would hire you as my chef."

That might be dangerous for the chiseled physique

I'm lusting after from afar. I keep this to myself. "Let me guess? Mom takes you to the buffets?"

"Mom is more interested in spa fare." He screws up his face. "As far as I can tell, that means no fat, no salt, and no flavor."

"There are more than a few decent restaurants around here," I point out, glancing toward the sparkling lights that glimmer in the night from all angles.

"That is true. I'll add that to my list of reasons why it's good to be back in Vegas."

"Back?" I perk up a little. Mr. Mysterious has slipped and given me a tidbit of information.

He sighs, tilting his head thoughtfully, as if considering how much he's given away. Finally, he nods. "From school."

"Oh, were you exiled? Stole daddy's t-bird? Knocked up the principal's daughter?" I rattle off options in mock horror.

"Do I get bad boy points if I say yes?"

I shake my head. "I've sworn off bad boys for lent."

"It's May."

"What can I say? I'm not Catholic. But the thing about bad boys is true." I'd dabbled in rebels with Hugo. That was enough to make me swear off guys like him for life.

"I'm back from college," he admits.

More information. I push myself up in my seat.

Things are starting to get interesting. "Where do you go?"

He hesitates, running his fingers through his hair. "Nowhere, actually. Not anymore. Tomorrow I get to tell my parents."

Way to go, Emma. How would someone who hadn't embraced the life of cynicism respond to that confession?

"Do you want to talk about it?" I ask slowly.

"Not really." His laugh is hollow. I recognize the bitter edge in it. Apparently Jameson and I are going to keep finding things we have in common.

"I have a knack for disappointing my parents, too," I promise him. "If my dad knew I was here..."

"Why are you here?" he asks bluntly. Maybe the time for games is over.

"My friend dragged me and then promptly left me to fend off Monroe's fury. I'm not supposed to be here." It feels good to admit it.

"Me either," he murmurs. "So neither of us want to be here and neither of us should be here. Tell me, Duchess. Who do you want to be tonight?"

I raise an eyebrow. "I thought I was the Duchess."

"If you like," he promises, "but tonight you can be anyone and anything. What will it be?"

"Carefree," I say without hesitation. "I want to be carefree."

Jameson falls silent as if considering my answer.

Studying me for a moment, he finally stands and holds out his hand.

"Another game?" he suggests.

"Twenty questions went so well for us," I say dryly.

"Truth or dare."

Narrowing my eyes, I take his hand and allow him to pull me up. "Truth."

"Why do you hate Monroe?" he asks.

"She stole my boyfriend. Truth or dare?" I don't linger on my answer. There's no way I'll get to carefree if I let thoughts of Jonas sneak into my subconscious.

"Truth."

"Why did you leave school?" I ask.

"I wouldn't call it a voluntary exit," he admits. "I was kicked out. This game sucks."

"Let's liven it up," I suggest. "Dare."

Jameson doesn't miss a beat. "Go swimming with me."

"I don't have a suit." My objection dies on my lips as he tugs his shirt over his head, revealing the hard slab of abs the thin fabric hinted at.

"Carefree, remember? Your turn."

I pause, realizing this might be a good time to gracelessly exit.

"C'mon Duchess. I showed you mine."

"Hardly a fair trade," I hedge, even as my fingers inch toward the hem of my skirt. "I'm only wearing this."

"That's the best news I've heard all day." A grin splits across his handsome face as my cheeks turn red.

"And underwear!"

"That's a shame," he says sadly, unbuckling his belt and sliding it through the loops. The sound of the leather vibrating against denim trembles across me. "Allow me to even things out."

I do my best not to gawk as his jeans hit the ground, but I can't quite help sneaking a peek at his boxer briefs. He taps his foot impatiently. "Do you need me to unzip you?"

I bite my lip before I nod. I barely trust myself to move at this point, let alone attempt the slightest change in position. Jameson circles around behind me, gathering my hair over my shoulder, he draws the zipper down. His hands slip under the straps of my dress as he pushes them down. The flimsy dress flutters into a pool of fabric at my feet as a fingertip trails down my back, between my shoulder blades, to the band of my bra.

I whip around before he can unsnap it. "It's going to take a little more than a dare to get me out of my panties."

He nods in acceptance, but I can see the glimmer in his eyes. I've just made this a challenge. The trouble is I'm not certain which one of us I want to win. He doesn't press it, though. Instead he grabs my hand and tugs me toward the water.

"It's a little bit chilly up here," I call right before he

grabs me around the waist and hurls us both into the deep end. Instinct kicks in and I struggle back toward the surface, but Jameson doesn't let go. Instead he smashes his lips to mine, and suddenly I don't need air. I don't need to fight. I go limp in his arms, my body molding naturally to his as the kiss deepens. He pushes us up, not breaking the kiss until we sputter apart for air. We suck in deep breaths, staring at one another. Water drips into his eyes from the strands of wet hair that have fallen across his forehead, but he doesn't blink as if he can't stand to break contact. Then he's kissing me again and I never want him to stop.

Jameson kicks against the water, moving us back until we hit the pool's tile wall. I don't protest as we spin around and I'm pressed against the tile. My arms splay against it as he moves between my legs. The thin fabric separating us rasps against my skin, urging me toward an edge I'm not ready to go over. He begins to explore my neck, his teeth and lips delivering thrills and shivers. When his hand moves up to cup my breast, he pulls back with a sinful smirk. "Any objection, Duchess?"

I meet his eyes, so silver in the moonlit night. He's gained the upper hand, but I have my own cards to play. My hand reaches between us to where our bodies are pinned against the wall, and rubs over the bulge trapped in his boxers.

"None at all," I purr, biting back a moan when his fingers slide under my bra. His thumb circles my nipple and for a second, I nearly lose the last ounce of control I have. Everything with him feels so good—so right. Mostly, because what we're doing and where we're doing it is so wrong.

That's what holds me back though. I'd been down this road before. It's landscape is a bit too familiar. Still, it's hard to turn the car around when we're zooming swiftly toward unknown territory.

"Truth or dare," I whisper through clenched teeth.

Jameson's mouth closes over mine, stealing my words, as if he's through playing games. Then, he pulls away. "Dare, I think."

I can't keep the smile off my face. That's what I was hoping he'd say.

6

DAWN creeps up on me. I blink against the sunlight before I sit bolt upright and stare at the unfamiliar surroundings. Memories from last night swim to the surface. Jameson's body pressed against mine. His hands gripping my wrists over my head while he kissed me until my lips were swollen. My fingers flutter to my mouth as I recall the vivid details of each hungry kiss. The towel draped over me drops to the ground and I scramble to grab it before someone spots my nearly naked ass waking up in the West's private pool cabana. In the light of day, it looks less glamorous and distinctly less friendly. But more than anything it looks empty.

I'm alone.

I look around for a note even as it sinks in that there won't be one. Two party crashers don't equal a relationship, I remind myself as I scrape up what's left of my pride. No note but my dress is neatly folded and waiting for me on the table next to my phone. It doesn't score Jameson any brownie points, but it keeps him in the neutral zone which is exactly where he belongs. Time to suck it up and do the walk of shame through enemy territory.

My phone vibrates with an incoming text and I grab it, but it isn't from Josie.

Mom: See you at 10!

I check the clock. 9:01. The right curse word hasn't been invented for this scenario, so I blurt all the other ones in existence as I tug my dress on. Gathering my shoes, I tiptoe back inside, praying to every god in history that Monroe isn't a morning person. I pass the dirty pots from last night on my way out, assuaging my guilt by reminding myself that the West's have a full hotel staff at their beck and call. The house is deadly silent, but I can almost imagine the orgy of passed out classmates I would find if I dared to return to the scene of the party. I'm smarter than to press my luck. The door to the study is ajar and I pause only long enough to feel stupid. There's no way Jameson is hanging around here.

"You could have woken me up," I grumble under my breath, but thinking of him recalls flashes of our night together. I'd almost given in to my desire but somehow I had clung to my integrity. The fact doesn't really take the sting out of waking up alone though.

Coming around the corner, two groggy faces greet me.

"Morning, sunshine," Hugo calls. Jonas just looks confused.

Taking a deep breath, I force myself to join them. Unless I want to go to brunch smelling like chlorine with raccoon eyes, I don't have the luxury of waiting around. Also getting the hell out of here seems like a pretty good idea.

"You are looking ravaged this morning," Hugo says. "Who's the lucky man? The bell boy?"

I keep my eyes trained on the glowing, down button. What is the point of having a private elevator if you have to wait?

"Shut up, man," Jonas mutters. "Hey Em, you need a ride home?"

I glance at the sliver of green left on my cell's battery status. I can't call Josie—even if she'd pick up. It will be dead before I can get an Uber. "I can take a cab."

"Don't be ridiculous. I'll drive you," he protests.

"What a gentleman," Hugo says. "First, you sleep on the couch and now you're offering rides to the peasants."

"A cab is not an issue," I say through gritted teeth. The elevator dings and Jonas holds the door until I wander inside.

"I insist. Hugo's headed to the airport anyway. I can drop you before I take him."

I open my mouth to protest, but Hugo butts in.

"Please, I will pay you to stop fighting him on this. I can't handle all the polite tension." He steps between us, folding his arms over his chest and watching the floor numbers descending. "So how was your evening?"

"I fell asleep." I'm not giving him more than that. An inch is more than enough for Hugo Roth to hang me with. "I was waiting for Josie and I got tired."

None of that is technically a lie, which means neither of them question it. The only way to salvage any of last night is if Hugo Roth never finds out that I nearly hooked up with some random guy in Monroe West's cabana.

"Josie was here?" Jonas asks slowly. "I didn't see her."

"That makes two of us." When I finally did find my prodigal friend, I was going to put a tracking device on her.

"Who's Josie?" Hugo asks, looking at both of us.

A sigh in disgust, but Jonas answers him. "She's in our class, man."

He shrugs, satisfied by this answer. That's all he needs to know. If Josie ever did make it onto his radar, he'd be all over her. That's just how guys are around her. The last thing I need is for her to trade in her daddy fetish for a dickhead phase.

"Why'd you even stay last night?" Hugo asks and I realize he's not talking to me. "After Monroe went ballistic like that."

"I wanted to make sure she was okay." Jonas glances at me. "She just gets anxious sometimes."

"I'd call that her permanent state of being," Hugo says flatly.

I barely manage to cover my laughter with a fake cough. For once I agree with Hugo. The elevator delivers us safely to the lobby before I lose my composure. A security guard waiting in front of it steps to the side as we exit, barely acknowledging us. I guess he gets paid enough to look the other way. Then again, everyone knows that Nathaniel West runs this city. No one would dare mess with his daughter's friends.

There are a sad number of people milling around the casino floor as we make our way to the valet stand. I'm not the only girl who didn't go home last night from the looks of it. Desperation mars the faces of those we pass as they hold their breaths as the wheel spins and the dice rolls. I can already tell what's in the cards for them. Being here makes me feel nauseous. I don't understand this world even though I know exactly how and why it works. But after years of finding dad passed out on the couch and the bank account drained, I'm no closer to comprehending what drives the obsession.

Why would anyone want to lose over and over again?

Hugo leans over as we wait for the valet to pull the car around. "Pathetic, isn't it? All that misery for a few minutes of high."

"That's easy for you to say." Contrary to convention, with the amount of money his family has, he can buy happiness. Or at least the equivalent amount of girls, booze, and drugs.

Before we can get into it, Jonas's silver Mercedes arrives.

"I thought Monroe wanted you to get a new car," Hugo says, grabbing the passenger handle. Jonas shoots him a meaningful look. "Oh, I see the chivalry continues. Might as well give her a little thrill."

Hugo opens the door and sweeps his arm out. "Your car."

They say what doesn't kill you makes you stronger, but what about what you don't kill? Because right now I need incentive not to lay him out on the pavement. Considering that I probably have about twenty minutes to get home, shower and throw on clothes, I don't have the time. I take a deep breath and steel myself as I climb into the passenger seat. We pull onto the Strip in silence.

"What's wrong with your car?" I ask conversationally.

"Nothing," Jonas says, flipping on the turn signal. "Monroe likes flashier cars."

Hugo leans forward, poking his head between the seats. "Maybe if she didn't make him sleep on the couch, he'd trade up."

"Put your seat belt on," Jonas barks as a cop car blazes past us, heading in the opposite direction with its sirens blaring. A few more follow.

"Another peaceful morning in Las Vegas," Hugo says dreamily. "This is God's country, I tell you."

For once I'm glad for their noise, anything to drown him out. Turning my attention out the window I stare past the people walking by and past the lights. In the daylight all I see is the trash littering the streets and the homeless man huddled under a collection of blankets.

"What a wonderful world," Hugo pipes up from behind me. I twist around to see him studying the same things I'm seeing, but I don't bother to respond.

The ride home is made all the more excruciating by the fact that Jonas insists on going under the speed limit while Hugo sings loudly to everything that comes over the radio. When I can't stand it anymore I hit the off button.

"I was listening to that," he calls.

"You can turn it on in a minute," I promise as we turn down my street. Dad's car is in the driveway.

"Are you going to be okay?" Jonas asks as he pulls in.

"Yeah, why?" I lie.

"I remember your dad was pretty strict about curfew."

I don't like that he remembers things like that. He has no right to hold onto any memories of us. "That was a long time ago."

"Okay. Have a good summer," he says as Hugo opens my door.

"Have a fun time at the pawn shop." He scoots into my seat, slamming the door in my face.

I wait for them to pull away, waving Jonas on when he hesitates. Was he always such a white knight? Hugo's right. It's a bit off-putting.

"That's the second thing you've agreed with him on today," I say aloud. It might be time to get my head checked.

On the off chance Dad is actually awake the last thing I need is for him to spot two boys bringing me home. When I finally get up the nerve to go inside, he's snoring on the couch with an empty bottle of Jack on the floor.

Saved by the booze.

I don't have time to feel bad for myself or clean up his mess, so I grab a blanket and toss it over him. Heading to my room, I strip down, trying not to think about last night. But undressing brings visions of Jameson flashing through my mind. I push the thoughts aside, plug in my phone and turn on the shower. There's no use, I'm going to be late.

The water feels good but it can't wash away the memory of his hands on me. I turn the faucet off with a groan. My neck is stiff from sleeping awkwardly last night and the last thing I want to do is go to brunch with my mom. But since being dutiful ensures that my tuition gets paid, I rummage through my closet until I find something suitably boring for such an occasion. Stepping into the yellow sundress, my phone begins to vibrate with a series of incoming messages. I grab a few bobby pins from the dresser and twist my wet hair up. It will have to do.

I don't have time to check the texts before Josie's ringtone begins to play. I lunge for it, hitting accept as I flop onto my bed.

"Where the hell were you?" I demand. "I looked for you everywhere."

"Me?" she shrieks. "I heard Monroe kicked you out. I spent half the night wandering through the casino looking for you."

Two ships passing in the night. Sighing, I cradle my phone to my ear and unscrew my mascara wand. "I texted you. I fell asleep out by the pool."

Now's not the time to tell her about Jameson. Not while it's still raw that he left me there like that.

"My phone died," she says quickly, "but that's not what's important. Turn on the news."

"The news?" I repeat.

"Emma!" Her tone is rich with warning, so I flip open my laptop.

"I'm online. What am I looking for?" I ask, still trying to do my make-up. Who says girls can't multi-task?

"Google West Casino," she demands.

A pit opens in my stomach as I key in the words and click on the streaming news link. Neither of us speaks as a reporter's voice comes over my speakers.

We're at the scene of a developing story. Authori-

ties have confirmed the discovery of a body in the penthouse of West Casino and Resort. The penthouse is the private residence of mogul Nathaniel West and his family. There's been no word yet on the identity of the victim but homicide units are at the scene.

"What the hell is going on?" I whisper.

"Who do you think it is?" Josie asks.

I don't know and that's what scares me.

7

ONE overpriced cab ride later and I'm no closer to processing Josie's bombshell. Today is not a great day to meet with my mom, but I've been summoned and apparently I take my duty as her daughter far more seriously than she takes her maternal obligations to me. Mariano's is packed with the usual late Saturday morning crowd of affluent 40-somethings. Perched atop one of Vegas's stodgier five star hotels, the restaurant offers panoramic views of the city. You don't get to a standing reservation here by playing slots. My guess is Mariano's clientele prefers to retain their view from the top.

Scanning the French twists and bad toupees I search for the pair that belongs to me, and then I spot her: Vivian Von Essen sipping a mimosa.

She used to be Vivian Southerly, but there's very few traces of the woman who used to be my mother.

My mom didn't bother doing her hair every morning. She couldn't afford the expensive dress suit she's wearing now. Mom didn't just trade in her husband, she traded in her whole life. Me included. All that's left of our relationship now is our resemblance. Someone once told me I'd be lucky to look like her when I'm older. Our green eyes are identical and we share the same sandy blonde hair. I'm guessing if I want my skin to stay youthful and radiant, I'll need more than good genes. Maybe I should get the name of her aesthetician and plastic surgeon now. I hear it's never too early to start.

I square my shoulders and mutter to myself as I approach her table, "Close your eyes and think of England."

She doesn't bother to look up from her phone. I clear my throat. I don't remember when I began feeling the need to wait for my mother's attention. I'm sure if Sigmund Freud was alive he'd be taking lots of notes. There's probably no one else who could sort out how twisted our relationship has become.

When she doesn't respond I clutch the back of the chair. "Good morning."

"Only for some it seems." Mom glances at me. "I'm just catching up on the news. What a nightmare!"

My smile is tight as I lean in to kiss her cheek. She doesn't know the half of it. As I straighten up I catch a whiff of Chanel No. 5. At least some things don't change. That had been a luxury she always found money for. Becca and I would sit at her feet while she applied it. She would place the precious bottle back on the vanity and tell us, "A girl may not have money but she can always have standards."

A waiter appears, startling me out of the past and into the present.

"I'll have what she's having," I say, nodding to her champagne flute.

She sets her phone down to shoot me a disapproving look. "Emma."

"An orange juice." I feign innocence that neither of us buys. If it comes as a cocktail Vivian Von Essen takes it that way. After last night I could've used a drink, but now I'll settle for shocking my mom into giving me attention. I think Freud had a term for that: desperation. "I didn't expect you to be in town this weekend."

Ice broken. Now to sit and endure the chill for an hour. I unfolded my napkin, which makes a shitty blanket, and wait for her to respond. That's how it is between us now: branches and cheek kisses and awkward small talk.

"You're starting your senior year. I thought that deserved a celebration."

At a place for lifestyle retirees. Gee thanks, Mom.

"There is something we could do if you're interested." Who knew an olive branch could feel so heavy? Extending it is exhausting, but thankfully she grabs for the metaphorical offering.

"Anything. This day is all about you, honey." She presses her lips together, no doubt trying to hold in her excitement.

Here goes nothing. "Could go by Becca's grave this afternoon? The headstone is up—"

"Let's not discuss that right now." She doesn't just cut me off, she dismisses the idea entirely. The interest she'd shown a few moments ago evaporates instantly, replaced by a distant, frosty demeanor.

That's all my sister—her daughter—is to her now: a subject that can be dismissed with one wave of a manicured hand. To my knowledge, Mom hasn't visited Becca's grave since we buried her. Then again given how much Valium she was on at the funeral, she hadn't really been present and accounted for then either. It hurts that I can't share my grief with her. Dad drinks, Mom ignores, and I pretend that I'm not walking around with a gaping hole where my family used to be. No one is going to be asking us to write a book on coping with loss anytime soon.

Meanwhile, she doesn't miss a beat. With a snap of the fingers a new morning-appropriate cocktail is on the way. "I thought we could discuss your summer plans."

"You know my summer plans already." I force the words past the lump in my throat. "I'm going to help dad at the shop and visit you in a few weeks."

"It's not necessary for you to waste your entire summer babysitting your father."

Actually it is if I want to have a house to return to this fall.

"I don't mind. I like an honest day's work." I can't resist the dig. Since she remarried my mother's occupation can best be described as economic developer. Show her a store and she'll help it stay in business.

But if she catches my none-too-subtle jab, she ignores it. "Filtering through other people's junk is hardly an honest day's work. You need to be focused on yourself right now, Em. With senior year coming up you should be thinking about extracurriculars, not haggling with your father's customers. Have you thought about what colleges you'll be applying to this fall?"

"Maybe Las Vegas Community College. I don't have a lot of options." I shrug, hoping that we can just pretend this subject away. Obviously Hans has been talking to her again. Until he came into the picture a few years ago, my mother's idea of a major was finding a husband. It can't be a coincidence that she's making other plans now. Although if I had to guess those plans still included me finding a husband, just one that would help her indoctrinate me to her lifestyle instead of the one I'd chosen.

"You aren't graduating from one of the premier prep schools in the country to go to community college. This is exactly what Hans and I are worried about." Her voice takes on a blustery tone, the one she uses to dismiss maids and bad foie gras. That means I've landed somewhere between the help and duck liver on her priority list.

I grip my salad fork and butter knife, because I need something to hold onto—something tangible and solid. Between dead bodies and college applications, this weekend is quickly becoming anything but relaxing. This is exactly what happens when you bypass Netflix in favor of living people. The only person who would understand isn't here. Her memory isn't even allowed.

"What are you worried about, Vivian? Having an embarrassment for a daughter? That would be a tragedy. Oh wait. You actually lost a daughter." I don't stop when she sucks in a pained breath, because I hope it hurt her. She needs to prove to me that she can feel something other than disdain and chemical dependency. "Did it even occur to you that Becca should be graduating this weekend?"

"Of course it occurred to me!" she snaps in a low voice. It takes a lot of skill to be pissed and still maintain your face in a crowd. "Do you think a day goes by without thinking of her? But Becca isn't here. You didn't die that night, Emma. I wish I could be discussing her college plans with her right now, but I can't."

So now what? I'm supposed to feel sorry for her. No freaking way. The utensils clatter out of my hands as I stand up in a rush, searching for the next way to needle her. Angry feels good. Vital. It's like a dose of adrenaline straight to my blood, and I can see it's having the same affect on her.

"Sit down," she hisses.

But maybe she's not ready to jump from practiced oblivion to all-consuming rage yet. I consider my options. I can storm out of here and hope it provides even more of a shock to her anti-depressant-riddled system or I can prove that I'm the adult she's afraid I'm becoming.

I sit down. Nothing rattles a parent's cage like fear.

"Accepting that she's gone might sound harsh to you," she whispers hurriedly, her eyes darting around the room to see if people are watching our little scene, "but it's the truth. I miss her, too. I've already taken two Xanax this morning. Truthfully, she is the reason that I'm here. I never should have left you two with your father."

"Is that why you want me to come to Palm Springs this summer?" I ask. Her guilt is misplaced. She shouldn't feel bad that she left us with our father, she should feel bad that she didn't want to be our mother anymore.

"Partially," she admits. Her new drink arrives and she clutches it like a security blanket. "Honey, you're a teenager. You shouldn't spend all your time taking care of your dad.

"Someone has to." It's supposed to be your job. Apparently my mother had missed the whole for richer or poorer line in her wedding vows. She might have been able to walk away from her marriage with no regrets but I couldn't give up on dad. He'd already lost one daughter.

"Consider it. I want you to have a nice time this summer."

I do, too. Working at Pawnography isn't exactly my dream vacation, but I'd chosen where my loyalties lay a long time ago. "With all the has-beens? Palm Springs isn't exactly a happening place, Mom."

"It's quiet," she corrects me, and she has a point. Vegas isn't exactly known for its calming presence. No, it's energy is exciting at best and frantic at worst.

It's one of the reasons I usually don't mind going to Palm Springs. Yes, the population skews toward senior citizen, but it lacks the stimulus overload of my hometown. Usually, I spend my time there each summer reading by the pool. Hans would stay in L.A., shooting dailies or overseeing edits so Becca and I could hang out with mom. We'd get our nails done and shop for the new school year. We stayed just long enough to pretend that our family wasn't a dysfunctional mess.

"I know your sister won't be there this year," Mom says in a quiet voice. I don't miss the slight tremble she's trying to hide. It's possible she's hurting more than she lets on.

That doesn't mean I can run away from my obligations here, though. "Exactly, I—"

She stops me. "That's why I need you to come."

"I'll be there in June like I promised, but I can't stay longer."

The prodigal waiter arrives with our breakfast entrees in time to soften my proclamation. I've never been so happy to see a stack of pancakes in my life. Across from me, my mother doesn't touch her chicken salad. Instead she stares directly at me, but her eyes remain vacant. Her mind is elsewhere even though she's sitting at the same table.

I cut into my food slowly, wondering if I should clap my hands or shake her. But after a few minutes, she blinks rapidly. Taking one look at my plate, she frowns. "Careful with the carbs, darling."

She's back. I pick up the syrup and pour more onto my plate. So much for the acting like an adult plan. If it means being as checked out as she is, I think I prefer to stay at my current level of maturity.

"Were you at the party at the West's last night?" She picks up her fork but doesn't bother to use it.

But it had the unsettling effect she, no doubt, hoped for. All the questions I'd left at the door when I came in race through my brain. There goes my appetite. "I thought we were avoiding morbid topics at breakfast."

It doesn't make sense to me that she's so desperate to avoid all mention of my sister, but here she is bringing up the latest scandal. The woman really should run for president. She knows exactly how to spin a situation in her favor.

"I cannot imagine what Evelyn is going through right now." There's an unusual amount of concern in her voice. Given our family history with the Wests, I didn't think she would care. Just like I wouldn't care if I hadn't been there last night.

If I hadn't been in the same house as a dead body and possibly a murderer.

"I didn't know you knew her." I try to sound casual even as my pulse ratchets up.

"Of course, I do." She stops, visibly adjusting as she corrects herself. "Or I did before I got involved with your father. When you take away the tourists this town is smaller than people think. I'd reach out but right now…"

Nerves get the better of me. I'd hoped to avoid the media circus, choosing to foolishly believe that what happened last night in no way will affect me. But most of Belle Mère Prep was at that party. The chances are decent that I know the person. "Did they say who died?"

Her eyes dart to her phone. I know she wants to check for the latest information but she refrains from picking it up. I, on the other hand, wish she would. At least this subject doesn't directly affect us, and it feels a lot safer than continuing to discuss Becca or college or my summer plans.

"Not yet," she says without bothering to check.

"Maybe it was Evelyn." I try to be delicate in my

suggestion even if I hadn't known until a few moments ago that my mother knew Mrs. West.

But the suggestion doesn't phase her. "She was out of town. Rumor has it that she prefers to make herself scarce when her children are throwing parties."

"Children?"

"Excuse me," our server interrupts, "can I get you ladies another drink?"

"Yes."

"No," I call over my mother, but she merely repeats herself with a smile.

"I'm the parent, remember?"

Maybe it would be better if both her and my dad had their parental rights revoked. Neither of them seem capable of healthfully dealing with their emotions. It's clearly setting a bad example for me. After all I went to a murder party last night.

"Speaking of, you haven't told me if you were there," Mom points out as if she can read my mind.

"I went, but I didn't stay long." Being put on the spot is making it difficult to come up with a story that doesn't involve skinny-dipping and making out with a stranger for most of the night. Instead I stumble upon a different, but equally true, excuse. "Monroe and I aren't exactly BFFs."

"I can't say I'm sorry to hear that. It's mercenary of me but I'm relieved that you weren't there. God only knows what happened last night." She sighs so deeply that I almost believe she cares.

My clutch vibrates on the table, alerting me to an incoming text, but I ignore it.

"Do you need to get that?" She eyes my bag.

"It can wait." We're nearly through with our meal. Then I can go back to my life and she can go back to hers.

"So Hans and I have been discussing your graduation present." Apparently she hasn't run out of ideas for small talk yet.

I raise one eyebrow. Is she getting me confused with Becca or does she just want to pawn off her present on me? "Getting a little ahead of yourselves. I have a year left."

"Well, we think you could use it now, especially because we both want to see more of you."

"Am I getting a pony?" I ask dryly. It seems fitting for the movie producer step-daddy to buy the affection of his wife's baggage with every little girl's dream present.

The smile creeping across her face is a little frightening. Maybe Hans isn't the only one who wants into my good graces. "Will you settle for a car?

"I don't think that's a good idea," I say quickly. "It's easier to cab in Vegas. Parking is so tricky and..." I'm blabbering now, because I know what's at the heart of my verbal diarrhea. To my surprise, she does, too.

"You weren't behind the wheel that night," she reminds me gently.

If I had been, we might be sitting here discussing

Becca's graduation present. She would have loved a car. I swallow the thought down into the pit of my stomach where I can bury it. "I know."

"Good!" Her concern vanishes, replaced by satisfaction. "It's being delivered later this week. Palm Springs is only a four hour drive. I'm always happy to send the jet for you, but if you ever need to run away..."

"I should run to my mommy?"

Her eyes crinkle at the edges and for a split second I'm little again and she's comforting me. "Yes, honey. You should always run to me."

I T'S a typical day in the Southwest—bright with a chance of sunburn. I ask my driver to let me off down the street so I can stop at the mailbox and grab the spam and collection notices that tell me I'm home. I've let them pile up for most of the week so I could concentrate on finals. Now ti's time to face the music, which I suspect will come in the form of a funeral march. The house is dark, which means Dad actually went to the shop: a small miracle that provides me a rare opportunity to open the blinds. Then I grab the empty bottle of whiskey he left on the floor and head toward the kitchen. Dropping the mail on the counter, I groan when the doorbell rings. So much for a few blissful moments to myself. It's high season for Jehovah's Witnesses in the city of sin. Truthfully, I think they come for the weather. I trudge to the door, bottle in hand. Might as well have some fun.

But the man at the door isn't in khaki slacks and his badge bears the emblem of the Las Vegas Police Department. He can't be more than a few years older than me, but he's obviously put a lot of a time into building his upper body strength to make up for the slight acne scars that mar his skin. His jaw is smooth, his hair cropped short, and he's sporting a classic pair of aviators.

"Emma Southerly?" The officer at the door nudges his sunglasses down on his nose to study me.

I thrust the bottle behind my back in a sudden fit of self-preservation. "Yes?"

He's either a saint or the sun temporarily blinded him, because he doesn't comment on it. "Would it be possible for you to come down to the station?"

"Why?" Apparently I've been reduced to simple questions. Up next: who, what, when, where. If I don't get myself together there's a breathalyzer in my future.

"We have you on a list of people who attended a party at the West's private residence last night. Is that correct?" His fingers hook into his belt loops as he sways impatiently. He already knows the answer. I doubt the security cameras all over the resort are props.

But since it's a good idea to cooperate with law enforcement, I nod.

"Have you been home all day?" he asks.

"No. I met my mom for brunch," I say slowly.

"Then I assume you heard that a body was found this morning at the West Resort," he continues, helpfully filling in the blanks as I try to comprehend that a policeman is standing on my front stoop.

"Yes, we discussed it over croissant." I refrain from rolling my eyes because I doubt he missed the sarcasm in the statement. "But I don't see what that has to do with me. Most of Belle Mère Prep was at that party last night."

This time he takes his sunglasses off and stares me down. "Most of them left before dawn."

"I bet you've been practicing that move for years. Did it feel good?"

His stare turns into a glare. Do not get on the bad side of Johnny Law.

"Okay, then. Do I need a lawyer?"

"Do you?" he asks.

He's taking this moment way too seriously, but I suppose most cops don't join the force to hand out parking tickets.

"Look if you want to call your parents, I can wait," he offers.

"No!" Calling parents equals my dad finding out that I willingly went to the Wests' house last night. "Sorry, I'm new to this. I think I've been watching too much CSI."

"Do you need a ride?" He puts his aviators back on.

I look past him to the squad car parked in my driveway. Thank God most of the neighbors work weekends. "Do I have to sit in the back?"

"Not this time."

"Okay, give me a minute." I back away from the door and attempt to surreptitiously deposit the bottle on the couch. Briefly I consider changing. Then again, I'm wearing a dress so I could just take off my panties and rock the whole Sharon Stone bit. This isn't how I saw my Saturday afternoon playing out, especially not the part where I fulfill some cop's wet dream.

"Get it over with, Emma," I mutter, grabbing my purse. As I head out the door I check his badge.

Officer Mobie.

"It couldn't have been easy to have that name in school," I say as he opens the passenger door for me.

He doesn't respond as he waits for me to get in. Mental note: bringing up childhood bullying might not be the best way to start conversation with the person putting you into a police cruiser.

I stare out the window, surprised when we pull into a small, residential station only a few blocks from my house. There are no reporters with flashing cameras or hordes of gawkers. Save for a few expensive cars parked awkwardly next to the force's Crown Vics, nothing's going on. Since it was a shorter ride than I expected, it didn't give me much time to prep myself for my first official police questioning. I'm sure that living in Vegas means it won't be my last. Not that there's much to sort through. Mostly all I feel is unfiltered dread and the need to pound my head against a brick wall. Bad things happen when I attempt socializing. When will I learn?

I study the Belle Mère Police Station before I turn and check the officer's badge again. Las Vegas Police Department. Is he lost? "I thought they found the body at the resort."

"They did, but the Belle Mère special crimes unit has been tasked with handling this case. We're assisting." Translation: since the situation involves people with money, it would be dealt with delicately.

"I'm guessing the media is camped out at your station, waiting for a press conference that isn't going to happen."

"I wouldn't know, miss." But this observation earns me the slightest twitch of the lips. I'm right and maybe Officer Mobie is human after all.

He escorts me inside. The waiting area looks more like the lobby of a nice hotel, complete with nondescript art and carefully selected, stain-resistant furniture. A receptionist with flame red hair pulled into a top knot shoots Officer Mobie a warm smile.

"Apparently she heard those school yard rumors about Mobie and his..." The look he gives me shuts me down. "So much for trying to pay a guy a compliment."

"Miss Southerly?" A tall woman approaches us as we near the elevator.

"Emma," I offer. I'm making all sorts of new friends today.

"Thank you, officer. I have her from here," she tells him.

I can't help but notice Mobie strutting over to the receptionist. He leans down and starts to chat her up. I love a happy ending.

"I'm Detective Mackey." She pushes the button on the elevator panel. "I apologize for dragging you down here on a Saturday."

Peeling my eyes from the fledgling romance in the lobby, I give her my attention. Mackey sports the typical blunt bob of a career woman with not much time to care about her hair and make-up. But her black suit is tailored precisely to her trim body, which means she cares enough to shop and exercise.

"It's not a problem. Bodies don't keep, do they?" I wince as soon as it's out of my mouth. Nervous humor strikes again.

To my relief, she ignores my tasteless joke. When the elevator delivers us to the second floor, she waits for me to exit. "Can I get you a coffee or a soda?"

"No thanks." I rub my palms on the skirt of my dress. The interview room looks like they stole it from a police procedural, and it's making my hands sweat. Apparently my body is feeling guilt by proximity.

The chair's metal legs scrape mercilessly against the tile floor as she takes the seat across from mine. "I'll get to the point. We simply need a statement from you about last night. Just what you remember and who you saw."

"Honestly, I didn't see much. I was being anti-social." Why does such an easy request feel so hard? I guess when you have nothing to hide, you have nothing to share either.

"Anti-social," she repeats, scribbling something into a black notebook. "So you were alone in the house?"

"No! I was with someone," I correct her quickly, even if having a partner in trespassing doesn't exactly make it right. "We just weren't at the party. We looked around."

And now I sound like I was casing the joint.

"Can you tell me the name of this person? I'll just need to corroborate his or her story. This is all routine. We need to get a picture of the evening's events and who was where." Her pencil stays poised over the pad of paper.

"His," I answer. If Jameson isn't already dealing with this mess, I'm about to throw him into the mix. I don't feel too bad, considering he didn't leave a note. "I only know his first name. Jameson. We were just hanging out. I made us some food in the kitchen and we went for a swim."

And kissed. A lot. I keep that tidbit to myself. It's fun enough admitting I made myself at home. She doesn't need the details of my sexscapades.

"I see." Detective Mackey pauses and makes another note. I crane my neck trying to read it. "Jameson. Do you know his last name?"

"No." I also don't have his phone number, I add

silently. Maybe last night wasn't as electric as I thought it was. Or maybe he'd been more drunk than I'd realized.

"If we showed you some pictures could you possibly identify him?" Detective Mackey's next question interrupts my analysis.

"Are you interested in him?" I ask slowly as realization creeps in.

"We're simply following up." Her face remains passive but her eyes study me. "Could you identify him?"

Jameson couldn't have anything to with this, but, honestly, the most I know about him is how his tongue feels down my throat.

"I got a pretty decent look at him." Understatement of the year. "I should be able to."

"Is there anything else you remember about that night? Anyone you saw?" she presses.

She's serious but I can't help laughing. "Are you kidding? Most of my school. Monroe's dad when we first came in. Some security guys."

"We?" Mackey perks up at this revelation. "Who were you with?"

"I came to the party with my best friend, Josie, but we got separated. She left early."

Which is why I'm here, and she isn't.

"So you didn't come with Jameson?"

"No, we met at the party. I've never seen him before last night." With all the circles we're running around this topic, I hope this counts as my daily cardio.

"Were you drinking?"

I'm surprised it took her this long to ask. Of course, that's what they would think, especially given that the whole party was a scene out of teens gone wild. It might be nice to blame my decision to spend the night making out with a random guy on tequila but I can't, even if she probably won't believe me. "Nope. All my poor choices are the result of my own stupidity."

She doesn't even smile, but there's probably not much room for a sense of humor in her vocation.

"Excuse me. I'll only be a moment and then we can wrap this up."

Rocking my chair onto its back legs, I study the room. There's the two way mirror that fools no one. Who knew that was a real thing? One window, a table, chairs, and four pastel green walls that are likely meant to be calming but just remind me of puke. Life on the inside isn't so bad. No worse than being stuck in a doctor's office. It's more purgatory than hell.

My gaze drifts to the hallway, waiting for her to return. A few people pass by and one stops. Jonas waves timidly at me from the other side of the glass. He's dressed in sweats and t-shirt, and dark hair is plastered to his sweaty forehead. I can imagine Officer Mobie rolling up to greet him at the lacrosse field. The sport is his one true love no matter what Monroe thinks. Jonas left this morning, too, which means they'll want his statement. Thank God Hugo is on a plane.

If Jonas was there, he might remember more than I did. I stand up and walk toward the door. Since he's so close to the family there's a good chance that he'll know more than I've been told, but as I reach for the handle, Monroe appears.

I shrink away. Not because I don't want her to see me, but because of how she looks. Monroe once came to a big lacrosse match with the flu and no one knew until she threw up all over the referee. She doesn't do public appearances without full hair and make-up. Today she's a mess though. Mascara remnants ring her eyes and her golden locks are thrown into an unbrushed ponytail. Jonas wraps his arms around her and she melts against him.

I've never seen her look so small or so vulnerable.

Backing up from the door, I accidentally catch her eye. She shoves Jonas away and points at the window. Detective Mackey rushes toward her, and although I can't hear what's being said, I can guess from the scarlet shade Monroe turns as she continues to yell. After a few minutes of enduring her mute, tonsil gymnastics, Jonas coaxes her away from the window.

Detective Mackey ducks back into the interview room, setting a file folder on the table. strait-laced. It's a state I like to call the Monroe effect.

"You have a fan," she says.

"We just love each other." I can only hope her

curiosity doesn't extend to more questions about my relationship with Monroe.

"She seemed confused as to why you're here. According to her, you were asked to leave the party." Mackey waits with her finger poised on the folder's edge.

Maybe I should start sewing my scarlet M now. Uninvited party guest? Check. Don't know the full name of my alibi? Check. Caught sneaking out by doting boyfriend? Check. I might convict myself.

"She did ask me to leave, but I got lost looking for my friend."

"That's how you met Jameson. Did he ask you to stay?"

"He's very persuasive." The truth is that he didn't convince me at all. He didn't ask me to stay with him or raid the Wests' pantry or swim in their pool. Thanks to him I'd left a trail of fingerprints that Hansel and Gretel could follow all over that penthouse.

"Can you tell me who this is?" She flips open the folder to a picture of Jameson. Just not my Jameson.

It's him, but not the boy I met last night. He's smiling in this picture, dressed in a button-down and pressed slacks, as he stands in front of a very expensive looking sports car. He seems happy but as I study the picture, I spot the distance in his eyes. They're vacant as if he's simply going through the motions. But the most puzzling aspect of the photo is that his arm is around Monroe. She's beaming at the camera, hugging him tightly.

"That's Jameson," I answer in a quiet voice, pushing the photo back to her. I don't want it to be the truth.

Mackey purses her lips and looks to the mirror on the other side of the room.

"Is someone behind that? Like on TV?" I wave at it. I've been here for over an hour and I have more questions than answers. I hope whoever is back there has more figured out than I do. "Do I pass the test?"

"Yes, you do as a matter of fact."

I turn back to her. "I was only joking. I tend to eat foot when I'm nervous."

"You're free to go, Emma." She puts the photo back into the folder and stands up.

"Wait. That's it?" I'd expected hours of grilling. Maybe a light or two shined in my face. Now she's saying I can just walk out of here.

She stops at the door and peers over at me. Distrust flashes in her eyes but she quickly hides it. "Unless you have something you want to tell us..."

"I've told you everything." I'm officially out of patience.

"We might need you to come in again. Please let us know if you'll be traveling." She opens the door but I just gawk at her.

"I'm going to see my mother in Palm Springs in a few weeks." I force myself onto my feet. The next question I have for her I don't want answered sitting down. "Am I suspect or something?"

"Everyone who was there last night is a person of interest." It's a stock answer that does nothing to assuage the panic welling in me.

"That's a very long list."

"Yes, it is." She gestures toward the door. Pulling out her phone, she taps the screen not bothering to look at me. She's through with me.

For now.

My head is still spinning when I step into the corridor. Before Detective Mackey can disappear, I call after her. "Detective?"

"Yes?"

"I don't even know what happened. Was someone murdered? Who? If I'm a person of interest, I'd like to know." This doesn't feel like an unreasonable request after answering all her questions.

"Yes, someone was murdered," she confirms as she clips her phone back on her belt. "At the moment, we're waiting to release that information."

"I guess I'll wait for the press conference." Nothing like being questioned for a crime you know nothing about.

Mackey presses her lips into a thin line. Not a smile or a wave or even a goodbye. When she's gone I slump against the wall. There's absolutely no way I'm asking for a ride home in a police car. I'm guessing that

Monroe isn't going to offer. More than transportation, I need someone to help sort through my feelings.

Emma: I need you to pick me up.

Josie: Sure. Where?

Emma: Promise you won't freak out.

Josie: Now I'm definitely going to freak out.

Emma: At the Belle Mère police station.

IT takes her so long to respond that I almost call to make certain she hasn't fainted. I'm going to wind up calling an Uber so I can go peel her off the floor.

Josie: On my way.

She'll have figured out why I'm here. It wouldn't take a genius to do that, but maybe a genius could sort out exactly what I've gotten myself into.

Footsteps shuffle closer and I discover Jonas clutching a Styrofoam cup. He holds it out to me. "I thought you could use this."

"I'm good." I fiddle with my phone for a few seconds, trying to ignore the awkward silence that's so obvious I can almost hear it. "Did you get a mug shot?"

"Um, no."

"Me either." I abandon my phone to my blackhole of a purse. "All those questions and nothing to show the grandkids."

Jonas chuckles and takes the wall next to me. It's odd being so close to him after all this time. It's been nearly two years since we broke up, and I've spent each of those days pretending he meant nothing to me. Today there's no flutter in my stomach or pangs in my chest. He's become someone I used to know.

I'd spent years thinking I loved him, and although I'd never admit it, even if I was being tortured, I wondered what would happen if he broke up with Monroe. But there's no electricity, no unseen force tugging me to him now. I guess I hadn't let myself get close enough to realize my feelings for him were an illusion. Now we're here and there's nothing to say to one another.

"So did you do it?" I ask conversationally. "If we're stuck together we might as well compare rap sheets."

"No!" Jonas stares at me, horror-stricken. "I would never hurt Monroe or her family."

I can't say the same when it comes to Monroe, but I bite my tongue. A police station probably isn't the best place to crack that joke. It might go over worse than saying the word bomb at an airport, and I don't think I can handle a cavity search on top of everything else this day has brought.

"I'm kidding," I reassure him. "I'm not even sure what they think we did."

"Us?" He tilts his head and a few dark strands flop over his forehead. "Nothing. They have a suspect already."

"Who?" I'd been right when I guessed he would know something. Now I just have to get him to fess up. Maybe I could borrow the interrogation room.

"Don't you know—" He struggles to find the words. It makes me want to draw him a map. If he's sitting on the answers to what's gone on in the last twenty-four hours I want to know. But before I can get anything out of him, Monroe rounds the corner and he does his best impression of a clam.

"What are you doing here? Haven't you done enough?" She marches straight up to me and sticks her face inches from my own.

I want to tell her to brush her teeth, but I take the high road. It's not a favor she'll ever return for me. She probably got woken up by a homicide squad this morning. Instead I cross my arms, pointing my elbows out in case she decides to move any closer. "I haven't done anything except crash your stupid party. I don't even know why I'm here."

I can take the high road but being nice to her is another story, even though this close I can see her eyes are bloodshot from crying.

"Don't play dumb. It makes all of us look bad when girls act stupid." Jonas grabs her hand but she shakes him off.

"Not acting, sugar. I really don't know," I inform her. Maybe I need to write clueless on a Post-It note and stick it to my forehead.

"You're not even worth yelling at," she mutters, sounding more tired than annoyed. She pulls away, turning her attention to Jonas, and grabbing my coffee out of his hands. Taking one sip, she scrunches her nose as if she expected it to be Starbucks. "That's terrible. They reached mom, so they said I could go home..."

She trails off as her voice cracks. I'm torn between wanting to melt into the wall and sneaking away. Watching your enemy break down isn't as thrilling as I might have suspected. It's just awkward. Right now I wish I was actually invisible to her, so that I could sneak out without prompting another round. She shakes her head once as if willing away tears. "Mom won't be back until tomorrow."

From now on I'm taking a vow of social celibacy. My only friends will be on my recommended watch list. Yes, I will miss out on nights like that night—and boys who can kiss like Jameson.

Jameson who might be a murderer, I remind myself, before I take a mental vacay down memory lane. Jameson who might be dead. It hurts to even consider it. But the truth is I don't know anything about Jameson, particularly why he was there last night, but Detective Mackey seems very interested in him. If my boy barometer is that off it might be best if I stay at home from now until the only thing that excites me is the local Bingo night.

"You can stay at my place. My parents are in

Maui," he says, rubbing her shoulder in a soothing gesture.

Yesterday afternoon it would have made me physically ill to be near this, but today I'm almost glad he's here to take care of her. It's as if I stepped through a funhouse mirror. Suddenly I'm over Jonas and worrying about Monroe. I need to get out of here before I join the pep squad and start wearing cardigans.

"I can't believe he actually did it," she whispers, obviously forgetting I'm still within earshot. "They didn't get along, but this? I have no idea when they're going to release Jameson. If they're going to..."

I take a step closer at the sound of his name, and Monroe's silver eyes narrow. "What are you looking at?"

But I'm not looking at her, I'm listening to her. "Jameson."

I don't know what reaction I expect to get out of her when I say his name. I simply can't help myself.

"Yes, you've helped him get away with murder."

Jameson. Murderer. The words crash into me but I don't feel them. They're as empty as the hollow pit left from where my stomach dropped out. I kissed him. I liked him. Until this moment, I'd mostly been able to dismiss all the strange questions I was asked this afternoon. Now the pieces are starting to fit, and as the whole picture comes into focus, I realize I'm in it. I'm not merely some girl who was in the wrong place at the wrong time.

"You don't know that he did it." That's Jonas—always the mediator. Would he still believe that if he knew that I'd woken up alone this morning?

Stomach acid bubbles into my throat and I swallow it—and the urge to vomit—down.

"Who else then? You? Her?" She shoves her thumb in my direction.

"They think Jameson did it?" I'm asking a question but I don't want the answers.

"Are you having some type of fit?" Monroe hisses, hurling a disgusted look my direction. "Yes, Jamie killed our father."

My family calls me Jamie. Everything clicks into place, and I reach out to steady myself against the wall. The photo of Jameson with Monroe. Everything Jameson said the night before. Jameson is Monroe's brother. Nathaniel's son.

Nathaniel is dead. Jameson is a West. And somehow I've found myself in the middle of a murder.

"You're here to be his alibi," Monroe continues. "I don't know what's more disgusting, knowing that a slut like you touched my brother or that he'd admit to everyone that he stooped so low."

"Monroe." Jonas says her name sharply, but I step forward and wiggle between them.

"Let her finish. She's been wanting to say this for a

long time." I'm tired of being used by the Wests. First my father was a pawn in Nathaniel's schemes and then I endured years of shit from Monroe. I hate them all, especially Jameson for using me to get himself out of trouble. All they do is take, and I'm about to give a little back.

"You never should have been there last night, but I guess I can't be surprised that you threw yourself at him. It's your typical pathetic move." She's practically spitting at me now.

"My typical pathetic move?" I repeat. "Like when you got Jonas drunk at the Freshman Desert Party and had sex with him on a car in front of half of the student body. Classy like that, Monroe? Because one of us is actually pathetic. There's a mirror in there if you want to see what she looks like."

Jonas looks positively constipated as I haul up this unpleasant memory, but hey it takes two to tango.

"Feel free to jump in any time or did she take your backbone along with your virginity?" I tell him.

"You know Hugo will be back tomorrow to give his statement if you need a pity fuck," Monroe steps in before I can unleash three years of anger on her boyfriend. "Sorry I can't be more help but I have to plan my father's funeral."

She drags Jonas toward the elevator, dumping the coffee cup on the floor. I suppose Monroe and her brother are a lot a like: they both expect other people to clean up their messes.

Brother.

The fight had been a welcome distraction from that piece of shrapnel that's now lodged in my chest about dead center. Jameson didn't know who I was last night, because he never would have touched a Southerly. Now conveniently I'm his alibi, which no one can ever know. It might kill my dad to know I was out all night with a guy, but if he found out that it was a West, he might kill him. And me. Belle Mère really doesn't need any more murders at the moment.

"Come on, Josie. Where are you?" Saying her name a loud works like an incantation because a second later the phone buzzes with a message that she's outside. I can't blame her for not wanting to come into the police station. If Detective Mackey is telling the truth and everyone at that party is a suspect, she'll get her fifteen minutes soon enough.

Texting her that I'm on my way out, I hit the elevator button. But as I step inside, the door next to my interview room opens—the one on the other side of the mirror. Jameson steps out followed by a man in a suit. He's dressed in his clothes from last night and a five o'clock shadow darkens his jaw. The hair my hands tangled through last night is a mess of coppery, brown tangles.

Because he slept with it wet. After our time in the pool. After we spent half the night with our bodies entwined. Did he sleep next to me? I push the thought as far back into my gray matter as I can, because if what Monroe told me is true, then he's dangerous. He pauses to talk to the man who must be his lawyer. Meanwhile the elevator doors are taking the length of a Bible to close. Jameson turns as if he can sense me watching him, and our eyes meet. A charge of electricity runs over my skin as he stares at me. The recognition and the hunger in his gaze calls my body to him while I scramble to press buttons on the control panel. His mouth opens as I stumble my salvation and the doors slide shut between us.

"YOU look pretty." Josie eyes the yellow dress I'd worn to appease my mom this morning. "Personally I don't dress up to go to the station, but to each her own."

I shoot her a look that says I'm not currently to be fucked with. Seeing Jameson ratcheted the warning level on my personal stupidity watch. I'd disregarded my instincts yesterday—a mistake I'd be paying for indefinitely.

When I don't offer any information, she presses forward. "Dare I ask?"

"Give me a minute." I close my eyes, squeezing them until spots of light appear. Then I hold out my arm. "Pinch me."

"What?" she asks.

"Pinch me," I request again. "I need to be woken up." A second later a sharp throb bursts across my skin, and I snatch my arm away from her. "I didn't really mean it."

"You asked me to do it twice!" Josie huffs as she puts the car into reverse and backs out of the parking lot.

For all intents and purposes, she did jolt me out of my hazy state, which is why I notice that her hair is frizzy like she just woke up. Today she's the one with the dark circles under her eyes and no make-up. She looks like how I feel. "Hey, you okay?"

"I was really worried about you last night." Her eyes stay glued to the road as if she's waiting for a chance to pull out of the station's parking lot, but the road is free of traffic. She continues, gazing blankly ahead, "I didn't get much sleep and then I've been watching the news all morning."

No. No. No.

"Don't work yourself up," I beg her. Last summer after the accident, Josie consumed every piece of media that focused on Becca's death. She watched the crash scene news video every night. She collected clippings from the paper. I even found a copy of the obituary stuffed inside one of her textbooks. When I confronted her about it, she admitted that none of it felt real. I understood that, and helping her through it had been easier than focusing on my own grief. I didn't want to see a repeat of that level of obsession from her again. "This has nothing to do with us, so you need to let it go."

She flinches at my gentle redirection, and her voice takes on a wild, uneven tone that mimics the screech of her tires as she pulls out hastily. "They aren't even saying anything on the news. And don't tell me it has nothing to do with us when I just picked you up at the police station."

"Turn here," I demand, pointing to the street ahead.

She swerves into the right lane and does as I ask, navigating to our favorite ice cream shop, Coffee & Cream. We pull into a spot and scramble out ahead of a large family in a minivan. For five blessed minutes, I focus on nothing but deciding what ice cream flavor to choose: a scoop of coffee and a scoop of tiramisu. But as soon as we both have cones in our hands, I'm back to reality. The outdoor patio is empty thanks to the afternoon heat. We might melt but we'll have our privacy.

"Spill," she says after a few licks of her mint chocolate chip. "Where were you last night and what were you doing at the police station today?"

I pause from my ice cream coma and give her a guilty look. "I stayed at Monroe's last night."

"Like a slumber party?" Josie asks in confusion, which quickly shifts to disbelief. "Did you two freeze each other's bras and practice kissing?"

Considering that I cost her a night's sleep and called her for a jail pick-up, I probably shouldn't have hit her with any more of the bizarre details of the last twenty-four hours so quickly. "I didn't stay with Monroe."

"Oh this is getting good!" she squeals.

"Eyes on the prize! For all you know I'm a murder-er," I remind her.

"I know for a fact that you aren't."

"How?" I ask, barely catching a drip of ice cream before it melts on my skirt.

"Because I know you," she says dismissively, "but you definitely were up to no good last night if you wound up at the police station. Just not murder."

I wish I had as much faith in myself as she has in me. Maybe I didn't kill anyone but I might have kissed someone who did. But the worst part is that after seeing him at the station, I know I would spend the night with him all over again in a heartbeat if I had the chance no matter the outcome. I'm not as innocent as she believes.

"It sounds like they're going to be pulling in everyone that was at the party," I say, not ready to delve into the psychological quagmire that my impromptu rendezvous has left me in.

"What?"

She pales a shade or two, so I hurry on. "I don't know for sure. It would take them forever, and they already have a suspect."

"Okay, you need to start sharing the details right now." It's a demand but the edges are brittle. Josie's nerves are clearly shot, and I'm not helping.

"I don't know where to begin," I hedge. Maybe going to her with this isn't the best idea. My best friend is as vibrant and carefree as a butterfly, but she's delicate like one, too.

But she's having none of it. Her lips purse before she releases a deep sigh. "How about you start with why you wound up spending the night at the Wests'?"

"I met this guy." I have to force myself to say it.

"How come stories of poor life choices always start that way?"

"More of your stories than mine," I remind her, even though Poor Life Choices should be my new band name.

"True. Continue."

"He was funny and sexy and a little arrogant, but it didn't turn me off." I might as well work through my feelings if I'm going to rehash all the details of last night.

"You can say that again," she says with a smirk. At least talking about a boy is distracting her from all the worrying.

"We didn't do it," I clarify. I'd given myself a nice checklist to meet before I got back in bed with a guy after my disastrous decision to lose my v-card to Hugo. At the very top of it: fall in love first. Cheesy, I know. But my mom is right about a girl having standards. "We just kissed and skinny-dipped and cooked."

Josie snorts at this revelation. "So you didn't do it,

but you cooked? You have a weird idea of what is supposed to happen during hook-ups."

"Thanks for the reminder. I'll ask your expert opinion next time—if I can find you!" I know she doesn't get why I keep my knees together but it doesn't really matter what she thinks on that topic.

"So what went wrong?" she asks, a note of impatience coloring her tone.

They accused him of murdering his father. I might need to break that to her a bit more carefully. "Apparently I really have a thing for bad boys."

"You've lost me again."

"Hang on." I pull out my phone and do a search for Jameson West; Google knows just who I'm talking about, I realize with a rush. I can't pinpoint if it's fear or excitement. I tap images and dozens of pictures flow onto my screen. Thanks to his father's high profile in business and his sister's brush with reality show fame, the Wests are Internet fodder. I hold up the phone so that Josie can see the photo. "Meet my latest poor decision."

"He's about twenty years too young for my taste, but I'd hardly call that a poor decision," she says with approval.

"Look at his name," I prompt. "I didn't know who he was."

"Wait, so if he's Jameson West and he was at the party that makes him...Monroe's brother? Did we even know she had a brother?"

"I didn't, but I'm not exactly President of the Monroe Appreciation Club."

She grabs my phone and scans the information. By the time she's done reading it, she'll probably know more about him than I do. "He went to military school and then attended Stanford," she tells me.

"That surprises me." I snatch the phone back and scan the short biography included on his father's Wiki entry.

"Nathaniel's son." She pauses and stares at me, completely neglecting her ice cream cone which drips all over her hand. "Holy shit, Em. Your dad is going to freak out."

"You can say that again." I brace myself for telling her the part I've been leaving out. "Nathaniel is dead. The police called me in to check Jameson's alibi."

"Did he actually do it?" she breathes.

"That's what I don't know," I admit. Part of me wants to say he couldn't have done it, even while the rest of me calls me out on my own BS. Two tiny voices have been whispering their opinions since we left the station, and I can't decide which one to listen to.

"What did your dad say?" she asks.

"He doesn't know, and I hope he doesn't find out." I know she won't say anything to him. I can't say the same for the rest of the world. How long can I really keep this a secret?

"As if this isn't going to be headline news." Josie

drops her unfinished cone onto a napkin and rubs her stomach. "I feel sick."

"Imagine how I feel. I made out with the son of my father's worst enemy, who also might be a murderer. I'm winning at life, wouldn't you say?"

"You didn't know." But that line isn't any more comforting coming from her. "So Nathaniel West is dead."

"Yeah. Monroe was at the station. I felt bad for her."

"Of course you did. You have a heart." Josie's head drops to my shoulder.

"Then I told her off for screwing Jonas," I add.

"You also have moxie. This is going to be a really long summer."

"I know. I've been thinking...maybe I should go to stay with my mom in Palm Springs." There's going to be media scrutiny. I could hope that my name wouldn't get dragged into this, but given that Nathaniel West consistently ranked in People magazine's most interesting people articles and he'd once been interviewed by Barbara Walters, it seems like a safe bet that anything and everything that has to do with his murder will get leaked.

"Will they let you?"

"It's not that far away." This morning when my mother suggested it, it was dead last on my list of summer activities right under 'take a pottery class' and 'go vegan,' but my stepfather knows a thing or two about nosey reporters coming from Hollywood. "It's my best bet not to wind up on the cover of every tabloid in America."

"What about Jameson?"

It's strange to hear her calling him that. Even if it is his real name. "What about him? We kissed. We didn't elope."

"That kiss dragged you into a murder investigation," she points out.

"Yes, no first date will ever live up to that one again."

"Did you talk to him?"

I shake my head, remembering how he tried to call out to me at the station. Part of me wants to hear him out, but what good could possibly come out of it. The police had a reason to suspect him. "I was in the right place at the right time. He needed someone to say he was busy during the murder."

"And you were busy," Josie waggles her eyebrows, and I elbow her in the ribs. "Maybe he really was with you when it happened. You should call him."

"I didn't get his number. I woke up alone with no note."

"Ouch!" Josie exclaims and I can already feel her sassy side coming out. "Never mind if he played you like that, let him fry."

"He did fold up my dress," I say in his defense.

"That doesn't make up for stealing the booty," she chastises me.

"He didn't steal the booty." I can't help but laugh at the indignation on her face. Now I remembered why I called her, because now that I've spilled my guts and we've faced the worst possible scenario, the whole situation is a lot less nightmarish. Time to return the favor. "What about you? Meet any prospective sugar daddies last night?"

"Oh look at the time." She holds up her bare wrist. "I have to get you home."

"You are avoiding the question," I accuse.

"You hate hearing about my papa bears."

"Oh that is gross!" I clutch my throat, pretending to gag.

"My point is made. I have to meet mom for dinner soon. Want to join us?"

I shake my head, recalling my vow to never leave the house again. "I think I'm going to stay home tonight. Going out with you gets me in trouble."

"Marion would never allow us to misbehave," Josie reminds me as I dump the remains of my ice cream cone in the trash. "That's why I'm glad she works nights." She winks as she unlocks her car.

"I think I just want to be alone. I know that sounds super pathetic," I add before she can state the obvious. "I need to think about stuff."

Like packing up and heading to Palm Springs. Josie doesn't argue with me. A few minutes later she drops me off at home. Dad's car is still gone and the blinds are only half opened since I got interrupted earlier. It feels like my whole day has been spent coming back to an empty house, and as much as I want to stew, I feel lonely looking at how quiet it is. Maybe being with mom this summer wouldn't be so bad.

The window rolls down behind me. "Call if you need me. I could be convinced to stay in tonight."

"Promise."

Inside, I stare at the fridge for a long time before I slam it shut. Nothing sounds good. The television binge I'd been planning seems a little less thrilling now that I've been pulled into my very own drama.

I spot the bottle I abandoned on the couch. I pick it up and deliver it successfully to the trash. The pile of bills from earlier gloat from the counter. Going to stay with mom might protect me from getting dragged into this any further, but it will also leave dad to his own devices. I pick one up and tear along the envelope seam, drawing out the letter, I nearly fall over. Three months behind on our electric bill. That means any minute the lights could go out. There's only one thing to do. An hour later I've sweet talked the utility company into letting me pay one installment. I hang up the phone and any thoughts I had of leaving Belle Mère along with it. I don't want to be stuck taking care of my dad forever, but I also don't want to lose my house.

Falling into an old routine seems like the most mind-numbing option, so I gather laundry. But even after listening to the whir and rumble of the machines,

I can't silence the inner debate bouncing around in my head.

On my way to my room with a basket full of folded clothes, I pass the door that's remained closed since last summer. This was Becca's house, too. With each day that passes, I forget her a little more. Stupid things like how her laugh sounded or the face she made when she was angry. All those tiny bits of a person that add up to a whole. I'm losing her piece by piece. I can't lose this house or her room. I need it if it's going to keep her memory alive. If Becca was here she would know what to do, and that's exactly what I needed to remember. Heading to my room, I strip off the sundress I wore for my mother and find a comfy pair of shorts and a tank top. Then I pull my hair into a ponytail and throw on my running shoes. I need to clear my head. I need to run. Not away from here but to someone. It's easy to forget that there's one other person I can always talk to —as long as I'm okay with her not responding.

11

I chose the Belle Mère graveyard because it was close to home. Dad wanted to be able to visit. But he visits as often as mom does. If I hadn't worried about it there wouldn't even be a headstone marking her grave. Maybe it would be easier if I could pretend she was just off at school or if I could drink away her memory, but I'd been cursed and blessed to spend the last few moments with her before she died. The run to the cemetery is boring, but it gives me time to clear my head. I run faster until my muscles burn and I'm drenched in sweat. I know I can't outrun what's happening, but that doesn't stop me from trying. By the time I reach the graveyard, the shade trees and green lawn are a welcome site. It's a bit strange to spend so much time and energy tending to the final resting place of the dead. In the desert, most of us don't get to look at green grass while we're alive. It's not comforting to think I'll be buried under it someday.

I jog along the path, reading names and dates. Nearly everyone here lived a nice, long life. They had decades on Becca. She didn't even get eighteen years. We buried her under a fledgling willow tree. A strange choice for Nevada, but rules don't seem to apply in graveyards. Reputations don't matter. Everyone here is beloved and missed and dear. Drought regulations don't exist or maybe the unnaturally green grass has evolved to soak up the tears of its visitors.

Becca's face greets me when I reach her site. Mom considered having her headstone laser-engraved with her image tacky, but I'd fought her on it. Her grave didn't need to suit anyone's taste but mine. It had been a good call. Over the last year, her photos began to vanish as her Facebook page was deleted and her Instagram stopped updating. Then they disappeared from our house, leaving only faded patches where they had hung for years. But it's even harder to think about all the photos she won't get to take.

Plopping down in front of the headstone, I give her a small grin. Her face beams back at me, locked in a happy moment from earlier that summer. It's one of the last pictures I have of her. My memory fills in the rest of the picture. Becca posing in front of a tall cactus, her red hair billowing behind her. She'll always look like this to me: young, happy. She'll never age, while

I've gotten older in the last twenty-four hours. I blink back tears. "Hey sis, have I got a story to tell you."

With Becca I leave nothing out. I tell her about sneaking around Nathaniel's office and meeting Jameson. I tell her that it seems impossible to have fallen in love with him a little bit in one night. I tell her that makes me feel stupid. Then I tell her it was all a lie. I ask her if I should go to Mom's and I tell her about Dad and his drinking. I know it's impossible but I can't help but hope that she'll speak up and offer me some insight. Although it would probably scare me to death.

I sit for a little while, soaking up how good it feels just to get it all off my chest, even though the only response is the wind in the willow branches. "I've never really thought much about what happens after we die, but I like the idea that you're listening somewhere. There's no way you landed the angel gig. It'll take you centuries before you work off all the trouble you made here."

As twilight falls in dusky hues over the cemetery, I stand up.

"I miss you, Becca," I whisper. I should have brought her flowers but I think she'd be okay just knowing that I brought her love. If I hurry I'll be home before dark, but as I turn I nearly jump out of my skin. Jameson's leaning against a tree. He's changed since I saw him last. He hasn't shaved but his hair is combed into neat chaos. In the dusky light, it's darker than I remember. His jeans hug his narrow hips but not as tightly as his shirt clings to his muscular torso. My thoughts flash to what he looks like out of his clothes and I blush. Striding up to him, I fold my arms over my chest and glare.

"How long have you been standing there?" I demand. Then a more important question occurs to me. "Did you follow me?"

"A little full of ourselves, Duchess." He shifts ever so slightly and I find myself doing the same.

Dammit, he is not who you thought he was, I remind myself.

"Don't call me that," I warn him. Did he think we would just pick up where we left off? That ship sailed when I woke up alone.

"Then I guess I'll call you Emma or would you prefer Ms. Southerly?" he asks, a chill runs so deeply in his words that I feel it in my own blood. Last night I thought he might devour me, tonight it feels like he'd settle for a mere mauling.

"I'd prefer you didn't call me anything." I move past him but his hand flies out and catches my wrist, stopping me in my tracks. I tug against his hold but he only tightens his grip. "Let go of me."

"We need to talk first."

"We needed to talk this morning," I tell him. "But I'm a little tired after spending most of the day covering for your ass with the homicide division."

"I appreciate that." But there's no gratitude in his face. He's reciting the obligatory thanks.

"I think getting someone off a murder rap deserves flowers or maybe chocolate," I bite back.

Jameson steps closer, still keeping my wrist pinned. "Did you think you got me off, Duchess?"

"You're using that word again," I warn him.

He ignores me. "Believe me, this is far from over."

"It is for us," I tell him.

His eyes flash, lightning in the stormy gray. I've upset him, which is a pretty stupid thing considering that he may or may not have killed someone in the last twenty-four hours. But as angry as I am at him, I can't find it in myself to be scared of him. Apparently reason, logic, and common sense have all deserted me for the time being. Jameson drops his hold on me.

"Why didn't you tell me who you were?" he asks.

"Oh, okay, Jameson West. Did you enjoy the part where I talked crap on your sister? Or when I basically said horrible things about your whole family? Let's not pretend we were honest with each other. "

"Agreed," he says to my surprise. "I'd suggest we start over. Jameson West."

He holds out his hand, but I don't take it.

"Emma Southerly," I say coldly. "We don't shake hands with Wests."

"That was our fathers' fight. It died with them."

"My dad is still alive," I tell him.

"Then he wins. I have no interest in continuing their petty feud."

"That's an incredibly enlightened sentiment, but not really one I share."

"So what do you have against the Wests, Miss Southerly?"

I hate how formal he sounds when he calls me that, but I can't exactly ask him to call me Duchess. Talk about sending the wrong signal. "My grief with your family goes back a few years."

"Ah yes. My troublemaker of a sister stole your boyfriend," he recalls.

"You were paying attention."

"I liked paying attention to you."

"Really?" I ask, "because I don't recall you leaving a note. Not very attentive, Mr. West."

"Check your phone," he orders.

It's in that moment that I realize it's sitting on the kitchen counter. I've ran all the way here without it. Now I'm talking to a murder suspect without a way to call for help. I might not be afraid of him, but I can't believe I was so stupid as to leave it behind. "I don't have it."

"You came all this way without your phone." Annoyance colors his disbelief.

"There was a time when people walked miles without cell phones," I remind him. Where does he get off treating me this way?

"Don't be cute, Emma. I can't allow you to run home."

"Excuse me?" I repeat, not bothering to hide my

shock. "Did we just jump through time and wind up in the 1950s? I'm not helpless."

"It's not safe," he ignores me, which only brings my rage from simmering to full boil. "You shouldn't be running without a way to call home."

"And it's safe to get in the car with you?"

"It's the safest place in the world for you. I need you alive."

A shiver races up my spine, but I channel my energy into convincing him to let me walk away. I have no idea what he's capable of, and I can never forget that. "I'll be fine if I leave now."

"We're not through talking."

"Listen, I don't know who you think you are—"

"I'm Jameson West," he interrupts me.

"That's so impressive," I mock him, "but I've been taking care of myself for a long time."

"You mean like staying out all night with men you don't know?"

"If by men, you mean you, then yes." Does he have some type of personality disorder? Dr. Jameson and Mr. West. "But it's not a habit of mine. I must have been suffering a bout of insanity."

"Then I suppose I was lucky," he says.

"You have no idea," I mutter. "You probably should have thrown a quarter in the slots. Luck was on your side."

"Others might disagree with you."

Oh, right. Dead dad. Whoops.

"I should go."

"Emma you can get in my car or I can follow you in my car. Those are your options."

My eyes narrow into slits so thin that I can barely see him. "Suit yourself."

I take off on a full jog before he can respond. Cutting through the gravestones, I narrowly make it to the street before a sleek, black BMW catches up with me. It slows down to match my pace, which would be comical if it wasn't so infuriating. I speed up my pace but it's no use. One, I'm not really much of a runner, so there's no way I can keep up that speed for long. Two, he's in a freaking car. By the time he's been following me for a mile, I dart right and take a side street. I have no idea if I can actually get to my house from here but I'm willing to chance it. The last streaks of daylight are fading into a milky blue sky as I quicken my pace. The desert is particularly dark at night and I have no desire to get stuck too far from home, especially with an inno-cent-until-proven-guilty murderer on my trail. But just as I round a corner, the BMW appears again.

"Do you even know how to get home?" he calls from the rolled down window.

"Yes."

"You're lying," he accuses. "Get in the car, Duchess."

"I told you not to call me that!" I yell between panting breaths.

"It seems to really suit your attitude at the

moment." He continues to idle alongside me. "If you get in, I'll drop you off a few houses down. If not, I'll be parked in your driveway before you can unlock your front door. Is your father home from work yet?"

I halt in my tracks. His scale of kissability to smack-ability just tipped heavily in favor of a backhand across his face. But he's hit the mark: I don't want to explain him to my dad. Reluctantly I jog around to the passenger side. The interior is sleek if a little bit utilitarian, but it hardly matters since he's turned the air conditioner on full blast. I want to pretend that I'm overheated from running, but his presence is also a contributing factor. My whole body turns traitor in his midst, remembering how his lips felt as they explored my skin.

But that was before I knew who he was or what he was capable of. If I couldn't bring myself to be scared of him, I could try to maintain some self-control.

"Buckle up," he commands me.

I grimace at him, abandoning the glorious chill coming from the vents and reach for my seatbelt. "I always buckle up."

"I imagined you'd say that, given..."

"Given what?" I press when he leaves his thought hanging between us.

"What happened to your sister," he finishes as he peels out of the neighborhood.

Yesterday he didn't know my name. Now he knows how my sister died? Uneasiness mixes with the Molotov cocktail of emotions I'm trying to suppress.

"How the hell do you know about that?"

"Public record," he answers with a shrug.

"Until today, you had no idea who I was," I remind him.

"I've done a little research. It probably occurred to you today that I might be guilty of my father's murder. I felt I needed to know who I was dealing with."

"And something you found led you to believe I could be pushed around?"

"Quite the opposite. As soon as I found out your last name, I assumed you'd be trouble."

He has no idea. "Look I told the police the truth, and that's all I'm going to tell them. I'm not adding to my story."

"I wouldn't ask you to." He frowns as if the suggestion that I lie is completely unpalatable.

"So you're just going to follow me now?" I ask him, "and look up news stories about my family and invite yourself into my life?"

"I'm inviting myself?" he repeats. He throws the stick shift into the next gear and speeds up until the engine roars. Now I see why he wanted me to put on my seat belt. "According to my sister, you weren't even invited last night."

I should have known this was going to come up, but it hardly seems like he has the right to be calling me out. "Lucky for you I crashed, I suppose."

"I couldn't agree more." He whips around a corner and I clutch the armrest between us. "You okay, Duchess?"

I shoot daggers at him. "Maybe you should slow down a little."

"Don't you trust me?" he asks.

"Really, this is where you want to go with this conversation?" Relief floods through me as we reach my street.

He switches gears, slowing down and coming to a halt a few houses away from my own. "Safely home, like I promised," he says. "You haven't answered my question. Do you trust me?"

I don't think we're talking about his driving skills anymore. "I don't know you."

"That hurts." The wounded quality in his voice speaks more to actual sincerity than flirtation.

"You let me believe that you were crashing that party, too."

"You believed what you wanted to believe." He has a point, but I'm not about to let him know it. He unbuckles his seat belt and twists to face me from the driver's seat. "I think you can let go now."

I release my death grip on the armrest, but I don't relax. His silvery eyes drift across my mouth. I feel them there as acutely as I felt his lips on my own last night. When his gaze finally reaches mine, I find the same questions there that I've been asking myself all afternoon. "Maybe I did," I admit slowly, "but I still didn't know who you were."

"I told you my name," he interrupts me. "You were the one playing coy."

"And you liked it," I blurt out.

A wolfish smile creeps onto his face, the wickedness reaching all the way up to those perfect gray eyes. "I did."

"Glad we've settled that." I tear myself away from his magnetic gaze and focus on the street ahead. Night has fallen. Most of the houses are still dark. Only a few lights twinkle from behind curtains, most of them left on to greet their owners when they arrive home from work or pleasure. People don't stay in on Saturday night in Las Vegas. We might be the only ones here right now.

"Looks empty," Jameson says, following my gaze.

I nod. In some aspects our worlds aren't so different. Most of the housers have house maids substituting for their parents who are too busy on business trips or entertaining clients or jetting off to some exotic vacation without them. It's the same here, even if it's on a smaller scale. My neighbors run small restaurants and grocery stores. They manage the casinos off the strip and in their free time, they pour their take-home back in to the Vegas economy.

"They're at work," I say aloud.

"Does it scare you to be with me?" He asks.

"No," I whisper. Admitting this to him feels like

opening a door that I might not be able to close. I chance a quick peek at him.

His profile is stunning in the moonlight that streams through the windshield, etching him in blunt lines and hard edges. He claimed that he had been away at school in California. The slight sun-kissed tone of his skin that glows faintly in the dim light suggests he'd been somewhere sunny, but he's not tan. Not like most of the people around here.

"What were you studying?" I ask before I can stop myself.

He turns to me looking a little surprised, but also pleased. "Business. No surprise, right?"

"You look like you didn't get outside much," I note.

"That seems a little hypocritical coming from you, Duchess, not that I mind." I flush at the appreciative tone in his voice, which only proves he's right.

"I buy stock in SPF 200," I tell him. "Even at the pool, I'm one of those girls with a hat and sunglasses that pauses her reading to slather as much sunscreen as possible. Skin cancer is a bitch."

"True enough," he says with a chuckle.

"I know I don't fit in here," I tell him.

"No, you don't," he murmurs. "You stand out."

"Is that why you talked to me?" I ask him.

"I spoke to you because it was rude not to acknowledge the fact that you were trespassing."

"Right." Embarrassment rolls over me in waves and I search for the door handle. That's all the reminder I need that I made a huge mistake wandering into that office, sticking around, getting into his car tonight. How many more huge mistakes would I be allowed before I had to pay the price?

He reaches across and grabs my hand. "I didn't mean it like that."

"Yeah, you probably didn't," I say, "but let's face it. I don't know you. You don't know me."

"I'd like to get to know you." I stopped trying to open the door and turn on him.

"Why?" If I discount the murder investigation focused on him, then I'm staring at the heir to a multi-billion dollar company who has the sense of humor to charm the panties off whomever he wants and the looks that mean he doesn't have to. He's the whole package. Compared to him, I'm nothing.

"Because last night I was more honest with you in the few hours we spent together than I've been with anyone my whole life and since then all I can think about is spending more time with you. I want to know you. Maybe I'm imagining it, but I think I've gotten under your skin, as well. If I'm wrong, tell me to leave, but if you felt even a hint of that last night, don't push me away."

"Would you let me?" I breathe. There's something about him that overwhelms me. I won't be able to let him in to part of my life. He'll simply consume me whole.

The hand gripping my own drops it, but only so he can reach up and cup my jaw. "Think about it."

My body leans forward instinctively, but his hand falls away breaking the spell.

"Okay." It's the most I can promise him. I throw open the door before he can convince me to change my mind.

"Duchess," he calls after me. I duck down to the open window. "Check your phone."

Jogging across my neighbors yards, I can feel him watching me from the car. He turns on the headlights to guide my path, but I don't hear the engine roar back to life until I step inside the house. I pause for a moment, catching my breath against the door, then I remember what he said.

My phone is waiting for me on the kitchen counter. Sliding it on, I search through the messages, but there's nothing there. What is he hoping I'll find? Then it hits me and I open my contact list. Skimming through it, I get to 'J.' He's typed in his full name. I select it and find a note written in the contact information. "Call me, Duchess. Please."

"What have you gotten yourself into?" I say to the empty kitchen for the two-hundredth time today. He's left what happens next up to me, but I'm not stupid enough to believe I have a choice. I should stay away from him. It's the smart thing to do. It's what I've always done, keeping my distance is a safe bet. Too bad I can't.

12

MONDAY, it's back to routine. I'm switching gears despite my dad's constant absence from work. Pawn shops thrive on their own in Las Vegas. There's always someone willing to gamble on their own treasures. Ninety percent of people don't come back, which means we have an unusual and original stock of junk for tourists to peruse. Nothing thrills a Midwestern farmer more than taking home a Billy Joel tour jacket. I've never claimed to understand it, but if it keeps the lights on and my stomach full, I can work with it.

Jerry is already waiting by the door when I pull into the lot. When I was a lot younger, Dad kept the place open 24 hours. He did some pretty good business considering he didn't mind taking items off drunk people's hands. He also got robbed a few too many times. Then Mom walked out, and he had to be practical, not that there weren't many nights that Becca and I spent sleeping on cots in the warehouse.

"Hey, Emma," Jerry greets me, holding out a Starbucks cup. "Cappuccino, right?"

"Jerry, if you're trying to get on my good side, it's working." I take the cup from him, and he starts to unlock the door. It takes longer to roll up the metal security gates than it does to turn on the computer, but there's little else that we have to worry about. The shop has a bookkeeper, a toddler could run a transaction. The rest is all instinct.

"Is your Dad coming in?" Jerry asks as I rearrange a pile of Star Wars memorabilia. I put Princess Leia in the front of the case because she's my favorite. I shrug in response to his question. "Your guess is as good as mine."

"I just thought maybe..." He trails off before he wanders away.

I'm not sure, but I think I make him nervous. I can't exactly blame him for assuming that I might know if Dad was coming in, but as usual I left him snoring off a hangover on the couch. The shop is closed on Sundays, and through some miracle Dad hasn't heard about what happened to Nathaniel West, which means he doesn't know that I was there that night. I guess Mom has been keeping secrets from him long enough that it didn't occur to her to mention it. Not that they're on speaking terms unless major parenting intervention is required.

I'd taken the coward's path and decided to stay in my room all day. We'd passed each other a few times coming in and out of the kitchen, but he'd been asleep before I'd put dinner in the oven. Usually I'd push it and wake him up, but I figured I'd better enjoy the calm before the storm. I have no idea when Jameson is going to show back up, but I have no doubt that he will. Eventually, even that will filter through Dad's alcohol-soaked brain.

By 2:00 pm I've bought a handful of old Beatles records and calmly informed a hysterical woman that her five carat diamond was a knock-off. I'd count it as a successful day except Dad still isn't here. Apparently, I'm going to be doing more than help out in the shop this summer. The melodic tingle of bells alerts me to a new customer, but when I glance up I find Jameson stalking through the entrance. I'm out from behind the counter before Jerry can greet him.

"What are you doing here?" I demand trying to sound more forceful than flustered and failing. I can't have Jameson showing up whenever he feels like it. He might not care about going toe to toe with my dad, but I have to live under the same roof as him. "You should go."

Jameson looks around at the store. Apart from the cluttered collections of pawned treasure, the place is vacant. "Is your dad here?"

"No." I begin to tap my foot on the floor. "He could walk in any minute though."

"Then we'll deal with that, if it happens." His tone is dismissive. What must it be like to never think more than ten minutes in advance? I guess he has the luxury to live that way.

Jerry walks over and eyes us suspiciously. He shoves his hands into his pockets, and puffs his chest out. "Can I help you with something?"

He directs the question at Jameson who merely looks at him like he's a bug that needs to be squashed. "I'm being helped already."

"Jerry, this is a friend," I say quickly trying to defuse the situation before Jerry picks up the phone. "He came by to drop something off. We'll just be a second." I grab Jameson's arm and pull him into the back room.

"This is interesting," he says as he takes in the stock of odds and ends.

Vintage toys sit forlornly next to unlit neon signs. In the corner, a dusty jukebox no longer plays music. He studies an old Monte Carlo half covered by a tarp. If the store is like a closet of junk, the backroom is a graveyard of sorts. This is where we send the items no one wants. "If there was a place on earth comprised of other people's treasures, this is it."

He picks up a Fender guitar. "I always wanted to take lessons."

I take it away from him and place it carefully back on the shelf. I don't even want his fingerprints in my world. "You break it, you buy it."

"Maybe I'll just buy it, Duchess." But he makes no move to pick it back up.

"Let's try this again, why are you here?" I'm rapidly losing patience with his air of mystery. It might have been sexy the other night, but now that the veil has been lifted, I know what's underneath: another spoiled rich boy who has the power to buy himself out of trouble.

"I wanted to see you. Isn't that reason enough?" he asks.

Considering our family history and the events that drew us together, it shouldn't feel like enough, but I have to work hard to keep myself from softening in his presence. He looks good today, as if that's news. Unlike the last time I saw him, he's cleanly shaven, and his hair is styled into that messy, wild chaos that begs to be grabbed onto. His grey shirt accents the silver in his tumultuous eyes, and there's a devious grin playing at the corners of his far too kissable lips. It's totally unfair that someone can look this good and be that rich too.

"You're staring at me," he accuses, but he's not put off. In fact, he seems turned on.

I look away quickly. "I thought you had something on your face."

His hand flies up to brush against his chin. "Did I get it?"

"No," I lie softly, moving closer. I brush my fingers along his smooth jaw. "Now it's gone."

Before I can pull back, his palm covers the back of

my hand, holding it against his face. "I wish it wasn't," he says.

It takes far too much willpower to draw away from him. If I could bottle up the amount it requires, I'd make a fortune off people who wanted to quit smoking or to lose fifty pounds. Maybe what they really need is a moment trying to resist him to see how much easier everything else in their life feels after.

"I want to take you out," he says.

"I'm not sure that's a good idea." I hear it coming out of my lips while my body screams yes. My self-preservation goddess is working overtime today. I'll have to give her a bonus.

My answer seems to surprise him. Then again, he probably doesn't hear no very often.

"I found what you left on my phone."

"Would you have called?" he asks me.

"Probably not when I saw your last name."

"And now?" he presses, taking a step towards me until our bodies are hovering mere inches from one another's. He's so close that I can smell the spicy notes of his cologne and feel the heat radiating off his body. My own remembers what it's like to have it pressed against it. An invisible thread seems to tug me in his direction.

I lock my knees and force myself to stay in place. "I'm still not sure it's a good idea."

"How can I convince you?" He steps closer again,

unknowingly doing a lot of the work. The nearer he comes to me, the more fuzzy the lines become.

"Maybe you should go," I suggest.

"If your dad isn't here, what's the problem with me being here?" he asks.

"He could show up." I'm on the defensive, and he doesn't even know why.

"Does he often not show up? I thought this was his place."

"Do I want to know how you know that?" I'm beginning to wonder if he's ordered a full dossier on my entire family. I'm not the one that needs a background check. "Dad hasn't had the easiest time," I struggle with what to say. "He has some issues."

There, that covers a whole range of evils, especially given the multifarious smorgasbord of vice that we reside in.

"Since your sister?" Jameson guesses.

I shake my head wondering only momentarily if he's distributed some type of truth serum to me. "Since I can remember," I admit, "some people handle their booze better than others."

"I'm prying," he says, but he doesn't apologize for it. I suppose given the amount I now know about his family, it's only fair.

"I've definitely pried into your personal life."

"Quid pro quo," he says.

"I thought you were a college dropout," I mock.

"I learned it from some girl I hooked up with. She was pretty smart."

"Are you attempting to flirt with me Mr. West?" I meander past him shamelessly shaking my ass a little as I go.

"I've never claimed to be a saint," stopping at the water cooler, I poor myself a Dixie cup full and sip it slowly. "Did you check your phone?"

"You're bypassing my question," I accuse him.

Refilling the cup I hold it out to him, "No Duchess. I just asked you a more important one. The answer to your question is obvious," he takes a drink, careful to place his lips exactly where my lip gloss smudged on the rim. I suspect it's not a coincidence, so does my body judging from how a thrill tingles through me landing with a burst of anticipation between my legs. "Yeah, I checked my phone."

"Then can we stop dicking around? I gave you my number, would you have called it before...?"

"Maybe if I found it. I suppose they might pull tricks like that in California, but where I come from, it's still good manners to leave a girl a note. Especially if she's still in her underwear. It's also considered polite to wake her up."

"You looked peaceful. I didn't want to disturb you." It's a half ass excuse, and one that does nothing to sway my opinion as to his innocence.

"Where did you go when you left me," I asked casually. I have to consider that there's a reason that

Jameson is the one the police are focused on. Even if I don't want to.

"Wrong question again Duchess. I think what you really meant to ask is did you kill your father?"

"We've been over that," but my voice peaks up a notch.

"Betraying the truth. It's okay if you don't believe me yet, but I'll give you my word that I didn't kill him, and someday that will mean something to you."

"Someday?" I raise an eyebrow. He's awfully sure of himself. Then again why wouldn't Jameson West be certain of his ability to sway the opinions of a woman. "Maybe you can start proving that to me by telling me where you were that night because you weren't there when I woke up."

"You want all the sordid details?" He asked. Anger contorts his face into a mask of rage, "You want me to tell you how I found my father's body? That I checked his pulse and tried to give him CPR?"

I take a step backward, needing to put distance between us as his voice continues to rise. But even when I do a magnetic force pulls me back toward him. I grab onto a shelf and brace myself, trying to break the power he seems to hold over me.

"That I was covered in his blood, and that, plus his will and testament make me guilty as sin in the eyes of the Belle Mère Police?" He's yelling now and I flinch at the brutal accusation running through his words. I'd brought this response on myself. "Or maybe you want to know about earlier when he came out onto the patio and found us there, and I pulled him inside before he could wake you up? Or about the argument we had after? If you like I can give you a timeline. It'll be an easier sell to the gossip magazines. Be honest, this is just another one of your little games. I only want you to tell me one thing."

"Is this what you think of me," I break in, choking back my own rage, "because if so, there's the door. Get the fuck out."

"I asked first." He ignores my request completely. Maybe I need to be a little less polite about it.

He leans so close to me that we're nearly kissing. "Are you looking for fame or fortune Duchess?"

I want to scream at him that I want the truth, but it's a little too A Few Good Men for me. Instead, I settle for walking over to the door and throwing it open.

"Out." I don't scream, I say it softly.

He strides past me, casting one hottie glance before he walks back into the store. I follow him out only to spot Jerry scurrying as far away from the two of us as possible.

"You get what you came for?" he asks Jameson as he walks toward the door.

"No," Jameson barks at him, "you have nothing I want here."

Jameson West is as hot and cold as a bad faucet. If I turn him on I don't know what I'll get. I spend the rest of the day replaying the conversation in my head, wondering how it got exactly from lighthearted banter to serious topics to accusations so quickly. But like everything centered around him, I'm left with more questions than answers.

13

A few hours later, I'm still fuming. I slam down the baseball card I've been analyzing and glare at it's owner. I'm not sure how he manages to keep his eyes wide and innocent underneath the bushy caterpillars that he calls eyebrows. Usually, I try to kill them with kindness. Even scammers often have a guilty conscious. Nine times out of ten, they'll grab their own junk and take off before I have to call them out. Sometimes they even apologize, but this guy must have brass balls. Too bad I'm about to hold them to the fire. "Wow. A baseball card signed by Babe Ruth."

I play dumb for a minute, simply because I enjoy watching the puppet dance. He leans against the counter and nods his head before he adjusts the collar of his tracksuit, "Yeah. One of my clients was running a little low on cash. He offered me this. I guess he didn't know what he had."

Okay, I didn't expect that. Now I almost feel bad for the guy. "What's your business?"

"Private investigator." He magics a business card out of his back pocket and hands it to me. "Dominic Chamber."

I suck in a breath and prep myself to give him the bad news. "Mr. Chamber," I begin, but he stops me.

"Dominic, please."

"Dominic, maybe you should stick to taking pictures of married men and tracking down lost puppies."

"Oh, man," he scratches the back of his head. "Are you telling me that's fake?"

"Yeah," I slide it across the glass to him. "Babe Ruth probably didn't use a blue Bic to sign autographs."

I could go into details about the Ruth's signature or how rarely he actually autographed something, but there's no need to rub salt in the wound. Hopefully, he stops accepting payment in the form of sentimental memorabilia.

"The card has to be worth something, right?" He scoops it up and studies it for a minute.

"Reproduction," I tell him gently. Why not tackle all the bad news today?

"Well, thanks."

"For what it's worth, I'm sorry. I wish it was real too." Even though I'm surrounded by authentic comic books and baseball cards, vintage guitars and more, ninety percent of what passes through this shop isn't real. It's easy enough to turn away the scammers, but far too many of the people who drag their treasures into us find out that they're clinging to another man's junk.

"Don't worry about it. I sent the guy the pictures he needs in an online gallery." He takes out his phone and swipes the screen a few times. "Poof. It's so easy to make evidence disappear."

Evidence; the word lands heavy on my chest. I do my best to smile, wishing him well. As soon as he's out the door, I notice he's left his card. I throw it in the drawer. You never know when you might need a private dick.

Checking my phone, I find half a dozen missed texts from Josie.

Josie: Have you seen this?

Josie: I'm freaking out right now.

Josie: You're totally hooking up with the world's sexiest killer.

I groan as I click on the link she sent me. Sure enough Jameson has been dubbed The World's Most Eligible Murderer. I guess it's time for him to have this fifteen minutes in this, outside the shadow of his father. The story mentions little about Nathaniel or the case the police are bringing against Jameson. Instead, it's a laundry list of complaints from Jameson's former college roommate. Most of it sounds like sour grapes, but I keep reading anyway until I reach the point where the roommate complains about the parade of women constantly showing up in their apartment.

Even though it's little more than musty laundry, I can only imagine how it feels for Jameson to read about himself in a national paper.

Emma: When did this story come out?

Josie: I saw it a few hours ago. It's trending on Facebook.

I scroll to the story's bi-line and check the publication information. The story was uploaded to the website this morning. Jameson had come to visit me after his former roommate, and I suspect former friend, served up a steamy dish of Jameson's secret sauce.

"You are so stupid," I mutter to myself.

"What's that?" Jerry calls from across the room.

I wave him off, "Nothing."

I choose to continue my chastisement in my head. Jameson had come here earlier to get away from the attention, but also because he seemed desperate to prove to me that he wasn't who they said he was. Maybe part of that desperation stemmed from having all his bad habits and mistakes on the front pages of papers at newsstands all over the country. It also explains the accusations he'd leveled at me, but it doesn't absolve him of what he'd said.

Josie: Need a ride?

I glance at the clock; two more hours. I shoot back a

message telling her to pick me up at 6:30 when the night manager will be in. Hitting the back button, my phone takes me to my contacts list. Jameson's name sits two slots above Josie's. I select it and hit the compose button. I can't seem to find the right words to let him know that I'm sorry and not sorry at the same time. Who knew being involved with a murder investigation made flirtation so difficult?

By 6:30, I still haven't come up with the right message. Waving goodbye to Jerry and the night manager, I flee the shop digging my phone out of my purse. I catch the faint purr of an engine idling nearby, but it's not Josie's beat up Honda Civic waiting for me. I don't even have to look up to know that. There's no screeching metal or flapping belts. Nope, this car sounds like it runs on sex.

I straighten up to face him. Jameson's lounging against the side of his car, against the side of his black BMW. He's not smiling, or frowning—or holding a weapon—so it's hard to get a read on his mood. "Waiting for someone?" I call.

"Waiting for you," he admits. His tone is still icy, but I shrug it off reminding myself that he's had a much worst day than me. "Need a ride?"

At the same moment, Josie pulls into Pawnography's parking lot. She slows to a stop when she sees the two of us staring each other down across the pavement. Despite what's happened to him, he doesn't deserve for me to get in his car. He doesn't need another free pass in life, but I can't look away. His gaze has locked onto my own, and the storm raging in those eyes when he left earlier has calmed. There's still so much I don't know and don't understand. He owes me answers. I turn toward Josie and gesture for her to leave. She doesn't need any more instruction thanks to best friend ESP, or maybe she defaulted to one of the unspoken rules of sisterhood and made herself scarce. She blows me a kiss before she circles around and heads back out. Shouldering my bag, I walk directly at him.

"Friend of yours?" he asks.

"Yep, and my ride home." To my surprise, he circles around the car with me and opens the passenger door. "You don't drive?"

I swallow against the raw nerves this question inspires. "I try not to."

Given what he knows about my family, he might be able to guess exactly why that is. He doesn't pressure me for answers. Unlike how you pressured him earlier, I accuse myself.

"Do you need to learn?" he asks. "I can teach you." We're changing gears before he's even released the brakes. Earlier he'd written me off as a gold digger. Now he's offering me private lessons. Maybe I could offer him one on not being a dick.

"I know how," I let my tone do the work for me. It's not really a subject I feel like getting into at the moment. I can't trust him.

Thankfully, Jameson switches subjects as he switches gears. "I apologize for earlier. Things have been complicated and..."

He leaves the unfinished thought hanging in the air.

"You don't know who to trust," I finish for him.

"You're perceptive," he notes.

If I'm going to earn a spot on his trust list and he's going to earn one on mine, now's the time to start being honest. "No. I read the interview with your college roommate today. He sold you out."

"The worst part is, a story like that might have got him some vacation money. I had Thanksgiving at his house last year, and he sold me out for a Mai Tai."

"Probably, an ocean view, too," I tag on. "Personally, I demanded they pay me in diamonds and sign over the Taj Mahal. I guess I have higher standards than him."

"I'm sorry I accused you."

"Look ..." I struggle with exactly how to put this, "The night we met, it was fun to play games. We both wanted to pretend to be someone else, but you're using my name to keep yourself out of jail. If whatever this is is going to work, you're going to have to start being honest with me."

"Does that work both ways, Duchess?"

I melt a little at the nickname. We're surviving our first unofficial fight, pet names intact.

"I have nothing to hide," I promise him.

He stops the BMW a few houses down, then he turns his flickering blue eyes on me. He reaches out, his thumb brushing over my lower lip as if considering this —considering me. "We all have something to hide, Duchess."

14

HEY Princess, I have a business meeting at the bank. See you later.

I pluck the post-it note off the fridge and shake my head. I hope he's talking about a meeting with an actual employee and not just an ATM on his way to the race track. Crumpling it, I check the clock on the microwave and curse. No time to make coffee this morning. Instead I grab a granola bar from the cupboard and dart out the door, stopping in my tracks when I spot Jameson's BMW in the driveway.

The low rumble of bass rattles his window as I knock on it. He turns down the music and rolls it down.

"Is this loitering or trespassing?" I ask.

"I call it chivalry," he corrects me. "Come on. I'll drive you to the shop."

I hesitate for a minute then I shoulder my purse and turn toward the bus station.

Jameson calls out again. "You're not going to walk all the way there."

Somehow I don't think he'd let me. Glancing down the street to make sure my dad is nowhere in sight I get into Jameson's car. All I'd need was for Dad to finish up his meeting early. But when we make it to the next block with no sign of him in sight, I finally relax in the leather seat.

"I wasn't going to walk," I tell him. I tap on the glass to point out a sign as we pass. "The bus drops me off down the street from the store."

His eyebrows knit together as if he's considering this. His hand drifts over and for one moment I think he's about to take mine but then he changes gears. "I know a pawn shop isn't a Fortune 500 company," Jameson says slowly, "but I'd think your father would be able to afford a car."

"He has one." I shrug, letting his judgment roll off my shoulders. It's a skill I've developed over the years.

"For you," he states the obvious.

"I don't want one." There, that's not a lie. I don't want a car. For a crazy second, I consider if my mother has arranged for Jameson to sway me into accepting my early graduation gift.

"You really shouldn't be taking the bus alone."

"Why? Because working yourself up over it screams first world problems."

He bypasses the question as he drifts effortlessly across lanes. "Do you take it at night when you don't have a ride?"

"Sometimes. Other times, Josie picks me up or Jerry takes me home."

"Jerry?" Jameson repeats stiffly.

"You met him yesterday," I remind him. Am I actually detecting a hint of jealousy in those broad shoulders? "The store manager."

Jameson relaxes with a laugh. "Oh, that guy."

I don't need to ask to know what he meant by that. Jerry's nice but he's not exactly a catch. The familiar melody of nursery rhymes builds outside the car windows. We stop at a traffic circle to yield to an ice cream truck, I sigh as it passes us.

"Do you want a popsicle?" Jameson asks and I realize I've been staring after it.

"Becca and I used to keep some money in one of those magnetic hide-a-key boxes under the mailbox. We'd run out as soon as we heard him coming."

"What did you get?" he asks.

"A bomb pop." I tell him. "I liked that it turned my tongue funny colors. What'd you get?"

"Me?" He shakes his head as if its a silly question, but I know better. A guy's favorite frozen dessert says a lot about him. "Nothing."

"No, when you were a kid," I press.

"Nothing," he repeats. "It's hard for the ice cream man to visit a gated community."

His answer tells me more than I expected. It doesn't take a talk show host to know that lack of ice cream means he had a sad childhood.

"You should have told me," I squeal, eager to remedy the situation now. "I would have jumped out and gotten you something."

"It's nine in the morning."

"You can read a clock!" I say in mock surprise. "Gorgeous and he can tell time. Where's the chapel?"

Jameson's eyebrow arches up. "Gorgeous huh?"

"I shouldn't have said that," I admit.

"Maybe we can catch the ice cream man another time," he suggests as he pulls up to Pawnography. "You can help me with my first time. Give me tips"

"You still have a first time available? I figured you'd handed all those out."

Relaxed Jameson vanishes, replaced by his rigid, distant alter ego. "Don't believe everything you read in the papers, Duchess."

"I don't," I rush to assure him. "But boys who kiss like you have had some practice."

The praise boosts his ego and puts the haughty smirk back on his face. "You could say that. I guess I saved one first to share with you though."

"Careful West, that's starting to sound like a date."

"We both know dates are off limits," he says, reminding me of the rule I had set. "Maybe I can sway you with a bomb pop."

I climb out of the car and lean down to look at him through the open window. "You can certainly try."

INVENTORY IS A WRECK. There's supposed to be standard procedure at the shop but with a constantly changing schedule and an absentee boss most of that's gone by the wayside. Items need cataloging and files need updating. I'm about to throw in the towel when a man in a white uniform approaches me by the register.

"Ms. Southerly?" he addresses me.

"Yes?" I'm not exactly fond of giving out my name these days, especially to strangers.

"These are for you." He hands me two cold, colorful packages.

Bomb pops. My pulse takes off like a rocket as I accept the treats.

"What do I owe you?" I ask him bending to grab my purse from the lower shelf, trying to ignore that my fingers are going numb from the ice.

"It's a gift from a friend," he says dismissing my offer. He refuses even to take the tip I hold out to him. "That's not necessary. He's a very good friend."

If only he knew the half of it.

I don't bother to hide my enthusiasm as I unwrap the popsicle and clutch the wooden stick. Holding up my camera I take a selfie licking it then I send it to Jameson.

Jameson: You're giving me ideas, Duchess.

Emma: That was unintentionally pornographic.

Jameson: Unintentional porn is my favorite kind.

My cheeks heat as I consider what he's thinking as he stares at my photo. I know what would be on my mind if he sent me a picture of his tongue, and it wouldn't be ice cream.

Time to change the subject.

Emma: Thank you for the Bomb Pop but what about you? Did you get one for yourself?

Jameson: No. I'm saving my first Bomb Pop to share with someone special.

Emma: Ice cream doesn't wait. It melts.

Jameson: Then maybe you need to reconsider going on that date with me.

I respond with another tawdry selfie with my lips wrapped around the tip of the popsicle. I'd said no more games but I might as well leave him guessing.

MY PRIVATE CHAUFFEUR service continues throughout the week. More than once I have to rush out the door before Dad sees that I'm getting a ride from someone other than Josie. The ten minutes to the shop and the ten minutes home have been the only alone time we've gotten this week since Dad decided to start making appearances at the store. At least it means I won't have to work on the weekend.

This morning, there's a cappuccino waiting in the cup holder for me. As soon as I pick it up I know it's dry with extra foam. Someone's been paying attention. I take a few cautious sips, but he's silent next to me. I almost always wait for him to speak because he's nicer in the mornings than I am, but today he's quiet.

"How was your night?" I ask.

"Uneventful." He doesn't elaborate further, but he dares to glance over at me. Dark circles under his eyes mar his otherwise perfect face.

My fingers twitch, and I realize I want to reach out and rub his back. I want to reassure him that everything's going to be fine, but that's not a promise I can make him. "Is your mom back yet?"

"No." Apparently he's answering in one word sentences today.

"How's Monroe?" This question earns me a genuine reaction.

His gaze flickers to me in surprise, a bemused grin taking resonance on his lips, "Do you really want to know how Monroe is?"

"No," I admit, setting my cup back down in the holder, "but I don't want to ride in silence the whole time either."

"She's begging me to talk to a psychiatrist, probably so she can buy my files and see if I did it. As if I'd walk into some quack and confess all of my sins."

Is there anything to confess? The question is on the tip of my tongue, but I swallow it down. The more time I spend with Jameson, the more convinced I am of his innocence, but that's when he's in a good mood. When he's happy it's as if the sun is shining directly on me—until a dark cloud descends. I can't always see it coming. More often than not, it has nothing to do with me. He arrives in these moods. Sometimes he loosens up, other times he barely cracks a smile. Each time I seem to pinpoint exactly how I feel about him, his mood changes, shifting as abruptly as an unforeseen storm.

"You know, there's one thing you can do to cheer me up."

I tilt my head in interest, "And that is?"

"Agree to go on a real date with me." He's not giving up on that. I should have known that's what he was getting at, but he finds a new way to ask everyday.

"I need time," I tell him. The air between us thickens, pulsating with negative energy. Forecast: hurricane. Category: Jameson.

"Take all the time you need." There's far more annoyance than reassurance in his statement. His knuckles are white from gripping the steering wheel so hard.

I groan as I reach for the door handle and swing it open.

"Wait," he calls. I swivel in my seat. Jameson catches my chin with his cupped hand, "Patience isn't one of my virtues."

"I can see that," I try to remain detached, but it's harder when he's touching me. My body craves that skin on skin contact. I want to melt into him.

"I'm trying," he says in a low voice that raises goosebumps along my arms.

I swallow and nod, at a loss for words. For one second I burrow into his hold, pressing my cheek against his open palm. Then I scramble out of the car before I give in again.

DAD IS A MAN POSSESSED. In the last week he's done more to organize product and file forms than he's done in the last three years. He tears through the store. Jerry and I stay out of his way. If he wants to work, neither of us are going to stop him. Gives me a chance to focus on the customers. It also means I don't have to close every single night and open the next morning.

Peeking into the back room I find him at the computer sorting through what looks like years of receipts, "You want something for lunch?"

"I'm fine." He doesn't look at me, so I step into the room and lean against the door frame.

"Need something?" he ask, his eyes crinkle at the corners as he beams at me.

"It's been awhile since I've seen you enjoy the shop so much."

"It's been awhile since I got good news," he admits to me.

"News?" I repeat. "You didn't share."

He leans in his chair, crossing his hands behind his

head, "I didn't have to honey. It's all over every newspaper in the country."

It takes a second for his words to sink in, but when I realize what he's referring to a hollow pang hits me square in the chest. "You mean what happened to Nathaniel West?"

"I know." He waves a hand at me. "It's morbid, but for a long time I'd stopped believing in karma."

"And now you do again," I finish for him despite my cotton ball of a tongue.

"What Nathaniel West did to this family is unforgivable. Do I have to remind you of that?" His mood slips for a moment, allowing me a glimmer of the hatred he'd wasted on him.

"You were friends once," I say in a soft voice. It had to count for something.

Dad shakes his head, rubbing the scruff on his chin. "You're too young to understand this, but sometimes people aren't who we think they are. Don't let your guard down, honey."

I want to tell him I've been understanding this for a couple of years now, but that I hadn't let hate consume me. I had allowed myself to be bitter, though. If I didn't get that in check would I wind up like him? Practically throwing a party for a dead man?

"You okay?" He studies me momentarily, but the wheels aren't turning behind his eyes. As far as he's concerned, I'll reach the same conclusion he has.

"Low blood sugar," I lie. "I think I'm going to go grab lunch.

"You're working too hard," he says with a sigh. "This is your summer, you should enjoy yourself. Grab lunch and take the afternoon off."

I mumble in agreement to this plan and back out of the room. Nathaniel West was my father's enemy. I'd taken that feud seriously, even when I didn't have a horse in the race. Now that the man was dead, that hatred had evaporated. Now my mixed feelings toward the West family had a lot more to do with the legacy of his children than the bad blood from before I was born. I hate Monroe, but I like Jameson. I can't take sides any more, and now, even my afternoon off feels tainted by the macabre joy my dad is taking in these events.

I dig my phone out and call Josie, but she doesn't answer. I could get an Uber or catch the bus... or I could call my personal driver.

It doesn't take me long to make my decision.

15

THERE'S not a cloud in the sky. It's bright blue, and Jameson is happy. I tuck the copy of *Wuthering Heights* I filched from the shop in my purse as soon as he parks his BMW. At least from where I stand there's no Heathcliff glower frozen on his face. But just like the wind on the moors, that could change any minute. Before I can shoulder my bag and head toward him, he's out of the car, opening the door.

"I'm starting to get used to this," I tease.

"Good."

"Is there any way we can stop at the store?" I ask him as he pulls out. I guess if he's going to insist on being my driver then he can help me run errands. "I need to grab some lunch stuff."

"Already taken care of, Duchess." He hitches his finger towards the back seat where a wicker basket sits.

"Is that a picnic basket?" I stare at it like it might disappear or transform into an everyday object. Because real life does not include hot guys and picnic baskets.

"I assumed I'd need to feed you," he explains. He assumed correctly. Somehow Jameson has managed to steadily out-number his mood swings with surprisingly sweet gestures.

"I didn't know picnic baskets were a real thing." I hope he didn't catch the slight break in my voice, even Yogi Bear didn't cry over picnics. It's been a long time since a guy surprised me with something as sweet as this. Actually, a guy never has.

"They are," he informs me. "It's just one of the many perks of living in a casino. I have a staff that can find picnic baskets."

"And make the picnics."

Jameson clutches his chest, shaking his head. "I'm wounded, Duchess. I made everything in that picnic basket."

"So you made me lunch, and now you're taking me where?" I search the scenery outside my window for a clue.

"That's a secret," he says.

"Secrets don't make friends," I grumble. "A picnic lunch and a surprise location? If I didn't know better, I'd think this was a date, but since I haven't agreed to a date, I can't possibly be right."

He blows off my none-too-subtle accusation with a

whistle. "This is just two friends having lunch. Don't read into things, Emma."

I check out his outfit for clues, but that hardly tells me anything. He's in his standard T-shirt and jeans. If Calvin Klein were a god, Jameson would be his muse. The shirt seems to caress his body and his jeans hang low on his hips as though his clothes were making love to him. It's enough to give a girl wicked thoughts. I squirm a little in my seat trying to squash my hunger. I doubt whatever he's packed in that basket will actually satisfy me down there.

Jameson weaves in and and out of traffic until the busy streets of Vegas are behind us, and we're on the open road. The desert slowly evolves into the peaks of mountains. I have no idea how far away from home he's taking me, and I don't care. As we climb higher, I start to spot scraggly pines and patches of snow. Coming from the desert to this feels like a fairy tale.

"Is this Mount Charleston?" I ask him, gawking at the vacation homes tucked into the mountainside.

He nods, his eyes glued to the winding road. "Have you ever been up here?"

"No. We've never made it." Despite the city's reputation, there actually are plenty of things to do outdoors. My family had just never done any of it. I'd like to say we're indoor types, but really mountains are just outside our comfort zone. Fresh air instead of lingering cigarette smoke. Scenery carved by nature. Not our scene. Despite the fact that the mountains have always been there hanging in the distance like an old film backdrop, they'd never felt real to me until now.

"What do you think?" Jameson asks, calling me from my thoughts and back to the reality of him.

I search for the right words to describe how it makes me feel. "They're magnificent."

"These aren't even great mountains," he confesses to me. "Someday I'll take you to the Appalachians or up to Colorado. We have a house in Aspen."

I press my lips into a thin smile. His family has vacation homes while my family's idea of a vacation has been jumping from one desert location to another for as long back as I can remember. "My vacations rely on the terms of a custody agreement."

"My family's vacations usually center around business. I don't know how you're supposed to break the cycle."

"Kill all the lawyers," I suggest.

"Right now, I'm a pretty big fan of lawyers." The conversation screeches to an awkward halt at the reminder of his legal troubles. It's as if there's a monster lurking in the room with us. Occasionally we forget it's there, then one of us slips up and reminds the other, and we're stuck watching our backs.

We lapse into silence until he turns down a rocky lane.

"Wow," I gasp. Tall trees flank either side of the drive as he zooms along to an unknown destination.

The road deposits us in front of a breathtaking chalet perched cliff side. I get out before he has a chance to come around and perform his gentlemanly duties.

The air is cold in my throat and its crispness makes my lungs hurt, but I drink it in greedily. There's no pollution or fumes tainting it. It tastes like pine needles and sunshine. I walk closer to the edge. Jameson gathers the picnic basket as I gawk at the amazing views. Vegas is a speck in the distance, and for once instead of neon signs and blinking lights, trees and rocks rise around me. When I finally turn away from it, I find Jameson standing a few yards away watching me.

"Is this your house?" I ask.

"Yes." His response is colored with a sadness I don't understand, and before I can reconsider, I cross to him and press my lips to his.

"What was that for?" he asks as we break apart.

"For sharing this with me," I tell him, "and because I don't want you to be sad here. Promise me."

He agrees to nothing. Instead, he gives me a half-smile and tugs me toward the house. It might be hard for a building to compete with the natural beauty of the mountain setting, but this house does. Jameson leads me through a living room that I can fit my whole house in, and out double doors to a back deck that jets precariously over the side of the rocky precipice. I wait patiently as he lays out his feast, trying not to laugh when he produces peanut butter and jelly sandwiches and a bag of chips.

"You're the gourmet cook," he reminds me, but his eyes twinkle like stars, reflecting some of my own amusement.

"No complaints. This is perfect." I unwrap my sandwich and take a large bite.

"It's crunchy peanut butter. I hope that's okay," he tells me as I begin to chew.

I swallow hard, nodding enthusiastically. "Crunchy is the best."

"Duchess, I think you're the peanut butter to my jelly," he says before he takes a bite of his own sandwich. It's a cheesy sentiment, but my stomach flutters.

When we finish, he hands me an apple. "Dessert?"

"There's a lack of frosting on that dessert." I scrunch up my nose. I guess even billionaire guys with model-level good looks can't get it right all the time.

"I'll keep that in mind for next time," he promises.

But I munch away at the apple, still mesmerized by the scenery around me.

"You know, I did come to the mountains once," I say, as I begin to recall a hazy memory from childhood.

"Didn't leave much of an impression," Jameson says.

I can't help but laugh as the memory grows clearer. "Actually, I think I blocked it out because it was traumatic. My parents took us on this road trip into California, and we went through the mountains."

"Road trips are the absolute worse."

Somehow I doubt that someone with a private jet

can actually commiserate with me on this topic, but I nod in agreement. Jameson reaches for my hand, entwining his fingers through mine, and I wonder if he can feel my pulse starting to beat frantically in my veins.

"What happened?" he prompts.

I shake my head trying to clear it before I continue, suddenly overcome by his nearness. "We brought my cousin, Ellie, along. I have no idea why. We had to stop to use the restroom. Mom told us to stay near the car, but we'd been cooped up for hours, so of course we started running around like bats out of hell. Anyway, I was racing Becca to a tree behind the rest stop. I'm sure it wasn't that far, but it felt like it at the time. I beat her there, but when I turned around, she was gone, so I ran back to the parking lot, and my parents were gone."

"What did you do?" he asks, trying to unsuccessfully stifle a laugh at my predicament. His thumb rubs circles on the inside of my wrist, and I have to take a deep breath.

"I sat down and cried," I admit. "I thought they left me because I wasn't listening to my mom. As it turns out, they forgot they had Ellie with them. All they saw was two kids in the backseat. It took twenty minutes of my sister raising hell before they turned around and realized she was trying to tell them I wasn't there."

"Were they angry at you," he asks, "when they got back?"

"No," I shake my head, feeling the slightest prick of

tears in the corner of my eyes as the memory turns from amusing to bittersweet. "I just remember my mom hugging me so hard, and then Becca grabbed my hand and promised she'd never leave me again."

I nearly choke on the words. Jameson drops his hold on my hand and wraps his arms around my shoulders, drawing me against his hard chest. How can he feel so sturdy and muscular, and still be such a soft place to land?

"My parents took us on a road trip once," he tells me, and I'm grateful for the distraction. "I don't remember much. Dad packed us all in the car and drove us out to this little city in California. There was a boardwalk and a giant ferris wheel. He gave us twenty bucks and let us play as many carnival games as we could. I'll never forget that city. It was called Heaven."

"Heaven?" I repeat in disbelief.

"Yes. Heaven is a place on earth," he says bemusedly.

"Did you ever go back?" I ask in a soft voice.

"No. I went to boarding school the next fall. Mom was convinced that military school was the right way to go."

"I can't see you at military school," I admit. "It actually seems more suited to Monroe."

"I don't think military school could handle Monroe" he says dryly. "But I tried to go back there once." His voice fades into the past, and even though we're pressed closely together, I can feel the distance of memory between us. "The whole town had been bought out. The boardwalk, the ferris wheel, the games. They were all gone."

"What happened to them?"

"Someone came in, developed everything into condos." He barks a hollow laugh. "I wasn't surprised when I found the project in my dad's portfolio."

Pulling back, I stare at him. "Are you telling me your father took your family on a vacation, then bought the place out, and turned it into senior living?"

"It's also very popular amongst young professionals," he says. "The city isn't even called Heaven any more."

"Did they rename it Purgatory?" I nuzzle into his arms, trying to think of the right thing to say. I'd thought my family was dysfunctional. But the Wests made my parents look like parents of the year. "If I had enough money. I'd buy a little town on the coast and name it Heaven."

"Could we build a boardwalk?" he asks.

"Oh, yes. Heaven has to have a boardwalk," I promise him.

"I like the picture you're painting of the afterlife."

"It's not an afterlife," I say. "It's just a dream."

Jameson presses his lips to my forehead, lingering there. It's a gesture filled with warmth and promises of its own. I want to stay here with him where everything is quiet and simple, and bad memories are only stories from the past. He buries his face in my hair and breathes in. Then, he speaks so softly that I barely catch it. "I hope your dreams come true, Duchess."

THAT NIGHT, I stare at the ceiling, unable to sleep. I replay every touch, every brush of his hand over mine, the few kisses we stole. Maybe tomorrow I can hang up some pictures of boy bands. I don't know what Jameson West is doing to me, but I know I don't want him to stop. I roll over and grab my pillow tightly, clamping my eyes closed, but nothing works. I'm still lying there when a soft tap catches my attention, followed by another. It takes a second to realize it's a rhythm. I go to my window and peek through the blinds. Two eyes stare back at me and I nearly jump out of my skin.

"Smooth," I muttered to myself as I tug on the cord so that I can unlock the window. "Trying to scare me to death?" I hiss at Jameson through the screen.

"I thought of something I wanted to ask you," he says.

"You could have tried using the phone." I crossed my arms and wait for his question.

"Why would I do that when your first floor window is so convenient? Come on, let me in, Duchess." He tosses me a crooked smile.

I glance over my shoulder at my closed bedroom door. "Have you lost your mind? If my dad comes in here and finds you, he'll kill you and he'll claim self-defense, *and* he'll get off."

"I'm not staying." He holds up two fingers. "Scout's promise."

"I doubt you were ever a Boy Scout." I pinch the metal tabs on the screen, wiggling it out of place, and set it against the wall.

Jameson ducks inside my window. Straightening up, he brushes off the dust from the window sill and looks around. "Not what I imagined," he admits.

"What did you imagine?"

"Something regal. Four poster bed. Hand maidens."

"We're fresh out of hand maidens," I say flatly. "I'm lucky if I have clean sheets on the bed."

The bed. The innocent thought has my eyes darting over to the rumpled sheets and comforter. Jameson's gaze follows mine in that direction. "Were you asleep?"

"No, I couldn't sleep. My head's too full." *Of you.* I keep that part to myself.

He holds out his hands. "Come here."

Now would be a very good time to share my parents' no boys in the bedroom rule, but the words stick on my tongue. It's easier to respect parental edicts when parents are around to enforce them. My dad might be home, but he's not really present. All I really have is my own instinct, and that's split decidedly down the middle on what I should do. The smart move is to show him the window. Instead, I take his hands. He leads me to the bed and I follow without objection.

But when Jameson kicks off his shoes, then he reaches for the hem of his shirt, my internal panic button goes off.

"What are you doing?" I whisper furiously. The only thing worse than my dad finding Jameson in my bedroom would be he finding a half dressed Jameson in my bed.

"I feel overdressed." He tips his chin toward me. It's at that moment I remember that I'm in a tank top and boy shorts. I try to tug my shirt down.

"No need to cover up," he reminds me. "I saw more than that on our first date."

"That wasn't a date," I correct him. "And before you get excited about the proximity of the bed, you should know that I have a checklist."

"A *checklist*?" he says like I've piqued his interest.

Why would I bring that up? Probably because I'm half-naked in my bedroom with him. "I, um, have a checklist before I'll have sex with a guy."

He's quiet for a moment before he runs his hand through his hair. "Duchess, are you a virgin?"

"No." Heat burns my cheeks and I pray he doesn't ask any more questions. "But, honestly, I made a huge mistake and I don't want another one on my record."

"Will you tell me what's on the checklist?" He grins widely.

"Absolutely not! You aren't gaming this system."

"I wouldn't dare," he promises. He drops onto my bed, grinning wildly and putting his upper torso on display. Instinct takes over and I crawl in next to him. Slowly he guides me to my side and slides his arm under my waist. My body molds to his, effortlessly. "What did you want to ask?"

But he doesn't answer. Instead, his nose and lips skim along the back of my neck, before he settles his mouth on my shoulder. The heat of his breath on my bare skin sends tingling emissaries of anticipation running through my body. "I wanted to know what you were dreaming about," he murmurs, "but you weren't sleeping."

"I was thinking," I say shyly.

"That's dangerous when you're trying to fall asleep." Anguish coats his words and I struggle in his grasp until I flip over to face him.

"Why aren't you asleep in your own bed?" I ask.

"Yours is more comfortable. I like this body pillow." He presses closer to me until I can feel *every* rock hard inch of him. Jameson wants me—his body betrays that much. I can feel the proof of it pressing into my hip.

I imagine what it would be like to let him slip between my legs. I'm not sure if it would help me sleep or keep me wide awake. Although something tells me that getting Jameson naked would make the night pass far too quickly.

But wanting him doesn't explain why he's here now. If it's company he's looking for, there's no end of women willing to help him out. He had come to me.

"And?" I press him. I refuse to be distracted by him.

"Nightmares." He leaves it at that.

I don't need him to tell me about nightmares. I know all too well how often the worst moments of your life revisit you in your dreams. "Sometimes I have nightmares about Becca," I confess to him instead. "It's like it's happening all over again and I can't wake up."

"You were there that night." It's a statement, not a question as if this is only now dawning on him. Wherever he'd gotten his information, it didn't include that little detail. "I'm sorry you had to see that."

"There's no use apologizing for life or tragedy. Both are inevitable."

Our foreheads press together and my breath falls into sync with his. "Maybe we're doing this wrong," he suggests.

"What?" I say in a sleepy voice.

"Strength in numbers, Duchess. I don't think I could have a nightmare with you in my arms."

"Then stay," I offer in a small voice before giving him my lips to convince him.

16

"I can't believe you're Jameson West's girlfriend," Josie says, as she sifts through the pile of clothes strewn across my bed. "I've been doing some research on him, and you're totally going to wind up on the cover of *People* Magazine."

"Or *US Weekly*, and I'm not his girlfriend," I grumble. "Is my navy dress over there?" The police department should consider hiring Josie to be an interrogator. Despite making Jameson promise to keep the status of our relationship a secret, I had spilled to her in less than two minutes. "No one's supposed to know, remember?"

"It's my secret." She pretends to draw a zipper over her lips. "Why is it a secret again?"

"Because my dad will have an aneurism if he finds out we're hanging out."

"Hanging out? Dating? Which is it, sister?" Josie demands.

"I don't know," I finally admit. Plopping onto my bed, I consider the question. It feels like my answer should be obvious. "I don't think I'm ready to be his girlfriend."

Josie groans as if she's half as frustrated as I am. "But you want to kiss him and practice making babies?"

"Maybe I should cancel." We both know that this thing between Jameson and I is a ticking time bomb. I pause at the mirror and mess with my hair for a moment, wondering if I should wear it up or down.

"You are not canceling," she insists. A moment later, she triumphantly holds up my navy dress.

It's one of my favorites since it never wrinkles. Plus its a simple A-line, but the second I see it, I realize it's all wrong. The simplicity I loved feels boring and uninspired now. I'll have to rip out my own tongue before I say it a loud but I want to impress Jameson.

"I think I'll wear jeans." Opening my drawer, I pull out a pair and shimmy into them.

"You're going on a date with a billionaire in denim?"

My eyes narrow in response to her disapproving tone. "I *can't* tell what you think of that. Jameson wears jeans all the time." And he looks good in them "Look, I know this is hard for you to believe, but for some girls, finding a guy they can hang out with in blue jeans and flip-flops is kind of a dream."

"Okay," she agrees, reluctantly. Her eyes flicker to the bag she brought with her. I haven't had the courage to ask what's inside. "As long as you realize there's a time and place for Louboutins."

"Between you and my mother, how could I ever forget?" I tease. I choose a soft black tank that flows to my hips, managing to achieve the pinnacle of lazy girl fashion: successfully mixing style and comfort.

"Just please wear these?" Josie begs, pulling a pair of strappy, gold Louboutins out of her bag. "It will dress it up just enough."

"No promises," I warn, but I hold out my hand. Slipping one on, I fasten it around my ankle and observe. It kills me to admit it, but it's actually kind of sexy.

"Oh, those are perfect," she squeals, clapping her hands like she got her birthday present.

"Where did you get them, anyway? You just started waiting tables." These shoes cost at least seven hundred dollars. I can't bring myself to consider dropping a Benjamin on new shoes. But even though Josie has a penchant for extravagance, she doesn't have the means to indulge her tastes.

She tips her chin up and rolls her eyes at me as if it's the most obvious thing in the world. "Do you really want to know?"

"A gift from one of your admirers," I guess. I try to block the vision of a drooling, forty-something business man blessing her with a shoe shopping spree, but even in my head, it can't be unseen. "Do you think I should spray these with Lysol?"

"I haven't even worn them yet." She pretends to pout as she flops backward onto my bed.

"That's why they're so tight." I wiggle my foot around before I take a few tentative steps. I wobble a bit but it's mostly successful. Maybe by the time Jameson arrives, I won't look like a newborn colt in high heels.

"I figured you could break them in for me," she says with a wink.

Josie oversees my hair, opting to gather it in a high ponytail and loosening just the right amount of hair to wisp around my neck. She digs out a pair of simple gold hoop earrings. I grimace as she hands them to me. "It's not too much," she reprimands.

"Okay, okay." I put them in and turn to check myself out in the mirror. I have to admit that I look good even if Josie's glam touches feel a bit unnatural.

"Fit for the arm of the world's most eligible ..." I shoot Josie a warning look before she can finish that statement, "...bachelor. You landed the whale, baby. Enjoy it."

JAMESON picks me up at home after my dad leaves. My heartbeat stutters like a scratched record when I glance out the front window and spot the black BMW idling in my driveway. When his face appears over the roof of the car, my stomach starts doing flips. This is why people write love songs. Maybe even why they listen to them. I'd never understood that before, but meeting him has opened my eyes to a world I'd turned my nose up to. Perhaps that's how he managed to sneak in under my radar.

I lock the front door and grip the handrail of our stoop as I brave the two steps. His eyes drift from my head to the expensive shoes on my feet. I blush a little as I brush past him.

"You can't argue with the name 'Duchess' now," he says to me before he shuts my door. I wait until he's in the driver's seat to ask why. "Because you look like a million dollars."

It's the oldest line in the book. Probably because it still works. I can't keep the goofy grin off my face.

"So," Jameson pauses as if he's struggling to get something out. "Do you trust me yet?"

I only have to consider for a moment. "Yes."

"Thank God because I wouldn't take you where we're headed if you didn't." I gulp at the underlying threat in his words. "I'm really sorry about this," he continues. "If there were any other way ..."

"Maybe I should stay home," I say slowly.

"You probably should, but I want to spend the day with you." If he feels sorry there's no regret in his voice. Instead he casts a devious grin at me. I shiver under his wolfish gaze. I'm not used to how he makes me feel yet, and I don't think I ever want to be.

But the thought that I might not get to spend the day with him makes me want to pout, but I reign in that impulse. "Look, if you have something better to do ..."

"No," he says, quickly. "But it is unfortunately something I can't get out of."

"Fine," I say before he can overthink our plans. "I'm in."

He doesn't wait for me to ask any more questions before he throws the car in reverse and speeds out of my neighborhood. "So where are we going?"

"To the airport."

"Are you supposed to leave the state?" I ask, before I consider an even more dangerous problem, "And I need to be back by curfew."

"We're not going anywhere," he says, tacking on, "this time." He takes the exit for the Las Vegas private airfield. We're cleared through security, and Jameson zooms toward this small outcrop of buildings that oversee the private runways high rollers use when they come to visit.

"My mom sends her jet here to pick me up for my summer trip." I tell him.

"What summer trip?" he asks in a strangled voice.

"I stay with her in Palm Springs over summer vacation." I don't miss how his knuckles tighten on the steering wheel as he processes this information. "I only go for a week."

The rigid tension in his shoulders doesn't dissipate. "Good to know. My mom's finally getting in. I don't trust a car service not to spill the details on her arrival. The last thing she needs to deal with is the press hounding her, so I need to pick her up and take her to our house on Mt. Charleston."

"I'm meeting your mom?"

"Is that a problem?"

It shouldn't be, but given the fragility of our connection, I hadn't expected to meet parents yet. Plus, we've known each other for a whole week. It's not like I'm buying bridal magazines, but I keep this to myself. If he wants me to meet his mom, it shouldn't be a big deal. "We just haven't had a real date yet."

"By my count, we've had several, Duchess." His mood lightens as he teases me, "But you say the word and I'll get us tickets to Blue Man Group."

I groan and bat him on the arm. "Don't you dare."

"Britney Spears?" he suggests.

"Getting colder."

"I hear Elton John might be coming to town." This time he's serious. He glances at me for approval, and I tap my nose and nod enthusiastically. "I'll look into tickets, but if we're not officially dating, then maybe I shouldn't be knocking on your bedroom window."

"That was a matter of survival. Neither of us were going to be able to fall asleep." At least that's how I sold that poor decision to myself. I bite my lip, remembering the dreamless peace I'd found thanks to his presence and the note waiting on my pillow in the morning.

"Sorry I had to sneak out like that," he says, as if he's reading my mind. "But I didn't want your dad to catch me."

"Probably smart," I agree. The shop has more than a few shotguns in its inventory.

"So are we officially dating or not?"

"Can I get back to you on that one?" I hedge. He doesn't say a word, but I see the muscle in his jaw twitch. A shadow descends over us as moody Jameson returns.

When the car is parked, he circles around to my side. As soon as I'm out, he grabs my hand tightly and leads me toward the edge of a runway. He doesn't speak as a small speck of a plane comes into view, barreling faster as it descends toward the strip in front of us. My hand is starting to hurt from his grip, but I don't dare remove it. As soon as the jet is on the ground, he yanks me forward.

Attendants rush over and open the door hovering nearby as a woman in a black wrap dress takes the steps. Her face is obscured by the brim of a large, black hat and a pair of oversized sunglasses. When she reaches the bottom, she takes off the glasses. Even from a few feet away, it's easy to see the red rimming her eyes. She's been crying, but when her gaze lands on

Jameson, she lights up. Her arms stretch out and he drags us toward her. "Jamie!"

"Mom," he greets her in a thick voice.

"Oh, darling." She crushes him into a hug, but he doesn't release my hand. I clear my throat awkwardly after a few minutes not wanting to feel like a third wheel.

"Maybe I should give you two a moment," I begin, but Jameson cuts me off.

"That's not necessary."

"I'm so sorry." Mrs. West opens her purse and pulls out a handkerchief, dabbing at her nose. She forces a smile onto her face. "We haven't been introduced. I'm Evelyn West."

I open my mouth to give her my name, but Jameson jumps in. "This is my girlfriend, Mom. Emma Southerly."

I can almost swear I feel the tarmac vibrate as the bombshells hit. It takes a concerted effort to stay on my feet. Girlfriend?

"*Southerly?*" His mother repeats in surprise, but she instantly regains her composure. "It's lovely to meet you. I'm so glad you've been able to be here with my Jameson. I just couldn't leave my father in his condition."

"It's okay, Mom," Jameson promises her. He loops his free arm through hers and guides us both back toward the BMW. "I have everything under control here."

She tenses when he says this. But if she has an opinion on the situation, she keeps it to herself. Jameson opens the front passenger door and drops my hand to help me in, but I shake my head. "I'm fine back here." I get into the back seat before he can protest.

"That's very sweet of you," Mrs. West says.

On the way to Mt. Charleston, she peppers us with questions. How did we meet? How long have we known each other? Jameson manages to skillfully answer them all without giving anything away. Now doesn't seem like the best time to mention exactly what party it was we met at or that our relationship was founded on an alibi. When we arrive at the mountain chalet, he carries her bag inside and she takes my arm as we head into the house.

"I'll admit I was a bit surprised when I heard your last name." She chooses her words carefully, but I can hear the edge to them. "Does your father know you're seeing my son?"

I consider lying, but then I shake my head. "No."

"Word to the wise, tell him sooner rather than later. Parents hate finding out they're being lied to." Her tone is gentle and I see now where Jameson gets his softer side as well as his looks.

Her eyes are the same silvery blue as her son's and her aristocratic features are the feminine equivalent of his brutal beauty. She removes her hat and I see that her hair is light like her daughter's, nearly white at the temples.

"I believe you know my mother," I say, looking for a subject of conversation while we wait for Jameson to return.

"How is Vivian?" she asks.

"Remarried living in Palm Springs."

Evelyn frowns at this revelation. "Do you see her often?"

"I stay with her during the summer. We split holidays. It's all very scheduled."

"A daughter's time with her mother should never be scheduled." She perks up as Jameson enters the room. "Speaking of, where is my daughter?"

"Probably with her boyfriend," Jameson informs her. "She's been shacking up with him all week."

"Are you two fighting?" she guesses, not at all perturbed by his implications.

"Considering Monroe thinks I did it, you could say that." A chill creeps into his words and I feel the urge to go to him and reassure him, but I force myself to stay still.

"Your sister is confused. This was traumatic for her and she doesn't know what to believe."

"She seems pretty eager to believe the Belle Mère Police Department." His broad shoulders go rigid with pent up tension and shadows seem to fall over his face, making it impossible to read how he's feeling.

"I'll speak with her."

"Let me know how that goes," he says coldly.

"I'm afraid my daughter and I have a typical relationship. I remind myself she's a teenager," Evelyn says to me conversationally, before redirecting her words to her son. "And we're all under a lot of stress, so we need to remember to be kind to one another."

He inclines his head. "Of course." His Adam's Apple bobs as he swallows. "I had the staff stock the kitchen. The maid should arrive tomorrow, so until then—"

"I do not need a maid," she interrupts him. "I'm perfectly capable of picking up my own laundry and cooking my own meals."

"I simply want to reduce your stress level," he suggests gently.

She looks to me with an eyebrow raised. "I think my son just mothered me."

"He can be a little controlling," I sympathize with her.

"I hope you fight him on that."

"Oh, I do," I promise her.

Jameson stoops down to kiss his mother's cheek. "Before you two conspire against me further, I should get her home."

"Do you have to go?" Evelyn asks. "I could whip us up a little dinner."

Jameson locks eyes with me and I can see his desperation to leave. I don't understand it, but I can sense it.

"I need to cook for my dad," I explain to her. "But some other time."

"I'm holding you to that." Before I realize it's happening, she's hugging me. This is way outside of my comfort zone, but I accept it because she's grieving and because she's my boyfriend's mother and because holy crap, Jameson is my boyfriend.

17

I'VE bypassed trust and gone straight to infatuation. My hand stays tightly knitted with Jameson's as he pulls into my driveway an hour later. Somehow he managed to steer and shift gears with the other as if he couldn't bare to relinquish his hold on me. Meanwhile, I'm still trying to wrap my head around the events of this afternoon. Apparently Jameson has made the decision about our relationship for me.

"I'm sorry that you had to spend the day stuck in the car."

But I shake my head at his apology. "It was nice to meet your mom."

"Said no girl ever."

"No, really," I say defensively. Meeting Evelyn West shines a light on the shadowy reputation of her family. After all the years hearing about the evil

Nathaniel West I'm beginning to question which party was actually wrong.

"What was your dad like?" I ask Jameson. He flinches at the mention of his father, and I immediately regret bringing it up.

"This is taking a turn for the worse if you're asking about my dad. Is it too late to take you to a movie?"

"I'm used to much more exciting dates," I tease him.

"Then you admit this is a date." There's a note of triumph in his voice and the feeling is contagious. Even though I'm the loser it makes me feel like the winner.

"I'm told I'm your girlfriend. What's with the label, West?"

"If it was up to me I'd actually plaster it on your forehead, but I'll settle for getting to tell people you're mine." He lifts my hand to his mouth and brushes a kiss.

How am I supposed to fight that? Sighing, I tug my hand free from him and put on my serious face. No matter what's happening between us, there are things I need to understand. "The only things I know about your dad is what my dad has told me."

"I imagine that's not good," Jameson says. "Dad was complicated."

Do they make father's day cards for complicated dads? I could imagine them sitting in the slots next to the empty spot for absentee fathers. *Here's to another year of never knowing how or if I'll meet your approval. Happy Father's Day.*

"He had this tremendous vision," Jameson's voice takes on a wistful tone that I understand. My voice sounds the same when I talk about Becca—half wishful, half regret. "He could see things other people couldn't but he was blind to what was right in front of him."

"Which was?" I prompt in a soft voice.

"A wife who was way too forgiving and two kids who just wanted his attention." Anger streaks through his words.

Empathy forms a lump in my throat. It aches there while I blink back tears. I'm used to my own disappointment when it comes to my genetic donors but they're both still alive. There's a chance I'll be able to fix my relationship with my parents. Jameson is going to have to live the rest of his life wondering what his dad really thought of him.

"Emma," he turns his silver eyes on me "Do you think I did it?"

"No." I reject the idea firmly. My lips form the shape of the word but no sound comes out. It's a truth that I feel deep within me. I don't need to speak it or claim it. I know he's innocent, because I've come to know his heart.

He clenches his eyes shut momentarily and when they open again they're flaming with a need that takes my breath away. Jameson reaches up and plucks the tie from my hair allowing my blonde locks to ripple down to my shoulders. His fingers rake through it gripping tightly as he smashes his lips against mine. There's a hunger in the kiss that I haven't completely felt since the night we met. It's been hiding in the background the whole time, but now we've unleashed it.

We fight closer. The kiss deepening as our tongues tangle greedily together searching for more. I want all of him no matter the consequences. My hand flattens on his hard chest. My heart jumps when I feel the speed with which his is racing.

He is my shouldn't.

My impossibility.

My can't.

And I'm not about to give him up.

When we break apart we pant for air pressing sweaty foreheads against one another. "I need to go," I say finally. "Dad will be home any minute."

"Maybe I should stay," he suggests.

"I think that kiss went to your head," I tell him.

"Emma, we can't avoid him forever."

"We can try." I trace an index finger along the curved lines of his abdomen. "We need a plan. Throwing this at him is the worst possible scenario."

He kisses my forehead and the sensation of his lips lingers there, making my head swim. "We'll discuss it tomorrow."

"You have a lot more things to worry about," I remind him. "Your mom is back now and—"

"I don't want to sneak around with you anymore," he stops me. His eyes sear into mine and the weight of what he's implying settles heavy on my chest.

How can I want to be with him and still be so afraid of the consequences? I lick my lips before I nod in agreement. "We can figure it out tomorrow."

I can still put the brakes on this before we make any stupid decisions like announcing our relationship to my dad. What's the rush to tell the world about?

"Do you have breakfast plans?" he asks pushing a strand of hair behind my ear. His fingertip grazes down my neck and it's all I can do to concentrate on what he's asking.

"Sleeping in. I'll probably get up for lunch."

"I like the idea of sleeping in."

I shake my head. "Sorry, my bed's invitation only tonight. The store is closed tomorrow. My Dad will be home all day."

Jameson leans forward slanting his head so that his lips hover over mine. "I really need to get a lock on your door, Duchess."

My core tightens at the thought of being alone with him in bed again. I haven't had time to go through my mental checklist but I'm pretty sure there are very few boxes left to mark. The pulse beating a war drum between my legs seems to agree with that assessment.

"Now get out of this car before I devour you," he threatens. His breath whispers over my lips before he pulls back and turns the engine on.

I practically stumble up the front walk and into the house. It's worse than drugs the effect he has on me but before I can turn my key in the lock, the door flies open. My dad glowers at me from the doorframe. His eyes flashing to the black BMW still idling in his driveway.

"Where the hell have you been?" he demands. The vodka on his breath nearly knocks me over and I move to shut the door but despite his condition he's too fast for me. He's on the front stoop before I can stop him.

"You get the hell out of here and stay away from my daughter," he screams. "I know who you are!"

"Dad!" I clutch his arm and try to drag him inside but he shakes me off so forcefully that I fall backwards. Jameson is out of the car in an instant. I shake it off and scramble into my feet to put a stop to this before it starts, but Dad reaches back and grabs a hold of my shoulder.

"What are you thinking?" he demands. "You can pack your bags. I've already spoken to your mother."

"I'm not going to Palm Springs," I shriek. I struggle to pull away from him but his grasp only tightens sinking into the soft flesh of my upper arm until tears smart my eyes. Jameson arrives and steps between us forcing him to release me. "You won't lay a finger on her."

"I am her father. I say who touches her and who gets the hell out of my house." He lists a bit as he directs his attention back to me. "Emma pack your bags. Your mother is sending the jet."

I step out from behind Jameson and regard him directly.

"No," I tell him hoping he can't see how hard my lower lip is trembling.

"I will not have another slut in this house. If you want to be your mom, you can live with her." He hurls the insult at me and it hits me square in the chest. After everything I've done for him, it takes so little to shatter my relationship with him forever.

"You won't speak about your daughter that way," Jameson sounds too calm as he continues to instruct my father regarding his unacceptable behavior.

"She's nothing to you." My dad turns his fury on Jameson pressing so close to him that their chests bump. "Don't let him fool you, Emma. The Wests should be studied by scientists. It's amazing how they can walk around without hearts."

"She is everything to me," Jameson interrupts him in a low voice. A thrill of fear ricochets through me as he reveals this.

I spot my dad's fist before Jameson does, and I jump in front of him in time to catch it in the stomach. The impact flattens me and I curl into a ball at their feet. Jameson drops to my side instantaneously.

"I need you to breathe, baby. I know it's hard," he says when I shake my head gasping for air that won't come. "Look at me. In and out." He demonstrates a slow breathing pattern and I suck at the air around me until I'm able to imitate it.

"Emma I'm so sorry." My dad tries to kneel down next to me. I see the tears on his cheeks but they mean nothing to me. Jameson shoves him away from me, knocking him onto his ass against the door.

"You don't deserve to look at her," he spits before he scoops me into his arms and carries me out the front door.

I tuck my body against his, willing myself to believe the reassuring words he whispers as he places me back in the passenger seat and buckles me up. I can't tear my eyes away from my childhood home. Dad stands in the doorway gripping it to stay upright. He looks defeated and small— and for the first time in my life I'm not sure I'll ever be able to forgive him.

18

JAMESON doesn't pressure me to talk as we head toward the lights of the city. I stare out the window, not processing the blur of life that we pass. Keeping my knees tucked against my chest, I try to ignore the tender ache in my belly. It's not really what's hurting me anyway. Dad didn't mean to hit me, but I can't erase the look of hatred on his face as his fist made impact. It was aimed at Jameson, but I felt his vehemence as acutely as I felt the punch. Without realizing what was happening, I'd started to see Jameson's problems as my own. If Dad hates him he might as well hate me as well.

I don't ask where we're going. I keep my mouth shut to hold back the sobs threatening to spill over. When we finally pull into the far valet circle in front of West Resort, I still can't bring myself to move.

He unbuckles my seat belt and patiently coaxes me

into his lap. I curl into a ball that he doesn't try to loosen. Instead he strokes my hair and kisses my forehead. He doesn't offer me meaningless words of reassurance or excuses for what happened. He's simply there, and that's all I need.

When my eyes are finally dry he tips my chin up with one finger, gazes down at me. I understand the look I see shining behind his blue eyes even though I've never experienced the feeling before this moment. The sensation wraps around me and I sense it doing the same to him, binding us together. Our lives become inextricable in that moment. We're inseparable and unbreakable. I'll carry his pain as he carries mine, and in these strong arms bracketing my body, I'll find protection.

"Do you want to talk about it?" he prompts.

"No," I croak, my voice still raw with the tears. He doesn't push it. We both know it was an accident, but accidents aren't always easily forgiven.

Out the window it begins to rain, which is as rare a thing in Las Vegas as finding true love. Both have been known to happen, just not often. The raindrops beat an irregular pattern on the roof of the car and slide down the windows like tears.

"I think we're stuck here," I say, finding my voice once more.

"If I'm with you I could be stuck anywhere." He guides my mouth to his and kisses me softly, then he sighs. "I know you don't want to talk about it, but I do need to know if you're okay physically. Do I need to take you to a doctor?"

"I'm not made of glass," I huff, but he won't let me pull away. "Believe me, I know that Duchess. You're far more precious than that. Gold, maybe? But even gold can be broken."

"He didn't mean to do it." I have to face this sooner or later. I had known there would be consequences when my dad found out about Jameson. I hadn't anticipated they'd be physical. Or that he'd throw me out. "He's sending me to Palm Springs."

"Yeah, I caught that." Jameson buries his mouth in my hair and silence descends over us once more.

"Do you have a house in Palm Springs?"

"I could," he says, but the playful tone in his voice remains flat. We both know he can't leave. Not while there's an active investigation into his father's murder, and he's the primary suspect.

"Who else would want to kill your father?"

"What?" He blinks in surprise at our rapidly changing conversation. I don't have time to explain that we need to figure this out. "The people here are toxic. Our lives are toxic. We need to get out."

"But we can't," he reminds me. "Not while they're investigating me."

"Did they tell you to stay in the city?"

He nods. "You?"

I shake my head. "They only asked if I was planning to leave this summer."

"I knew they didn't suspect you." There's a finality to his tone that leaves me confused. His eyes drop down, and when he looks up they're full of regret. "Have you ever needed to tell someone something even though it might ruin everything?"

I suck in a breath. "That doesn't sound like a hypothetical question."

"It's not."

"Should I get back in my own seat for this?" I ask him.

"I'd rather keep my hands on you for as long as possible." Uh-oh. Whatever is about to come out of his mouth has the potential to change everything. "I was in the other room when they questioned you the day we found his body."

I nod. I'd seen him coming out as I got into the elevator. It didn't take a membership in MENSA to know why he'd been next door. "When they wanted me to corroborate your alibi?"

"Yes." He pauses before adding on, "and no. You have to understand, you were this mysterious girl who showed up and was lurking around the house. I liked you. I really did, but it would have been stupid of me not to mention you to the police."

"Wait. What are you saying?" I pry myself from his grasp, and even though there's very little wiggle room I pull away until the steering wheel digs into my shoulder blades.

"I told him just that. That I'd found a girl in my

dad's study who wouldn't tell me her name, and that she'd stayed the whole night."

"How did you know I stayed?" I asked angrily. "Because you weren't with me."

"After I left you on the patio, I went to speak to my dad. We had words. He handled me leaving Stanford as well as you might expect. After that I found a bottle of whiskey and made a new friend for a couple of hours. Sometimes darkness overcomes me, Emma. It's not something I like about myself, but I can't deny it. I left you out there because I couldn't bear for you to see me like this. Then I saw you leaving with Jonas and Hugo, and I knew Monroe would be able to tell me who you were."

"You wanted to know who I was?" I ask, softening too much.

"I wanted to run after you but I stopped myself."

"Why?" I demand. The question covers so many unanswered things from that night.

"I'd been drinking for hours. I passed out with my head on the bar. It wasn't a proud moment for me."

"And then you found your dad." My stomach begins to churn as I relive the night with him. I don't like experiencing it through his eyes.

"Yes, and I didn't think. I tried to stop the bleeding and checked his pulse. Then I realized it was too late. Monroe found me like that: covered in his blood and drunk off my ass. She called the cops. All I can remember is her screaming 'what did you do?' over and over again. She couldn't hear a word I was saying. She still can't.

"So, when the police brought you in, I told them about the girl," he repeats himself. "I let them draw their own conclusions. You were my alibi."

"But I was also your primary suspect," I guess. Betrayal rips my heart in half, and my hand flies to my mouth to hold back a sob, but Jameson won't let me scramble away from him. He grabs me by the hips and holds me on his lap. "The day in the cemetery when I found you, you didn't trust me. You suspected I might have killed him. Am I right?"

I force myself to nod.

"But you didn't want that to be the case," he continues.

I nod again.

"That's exactly how I felt the whole time," he says. "I needed to find out if I could trust you. I needed to find out who you were. As soon as Monroe told me you were a Southerly, it was a strike against you."

"The feeling's mutual," I spit at him.

"Calm down, Duchess," he urges me, but I dodge his hand when he tries to stroke my cheek. "I stood there and listened to you talking to your sister in the graveyard, and I knew then that you could never hurt anyone."

"But you had to be sure, I guess."

"It sounds like you're familiar with the stakes."

"I am," I admit slowly. I want to be angry at him for

suspecting me. This whole time he had been putting me to the test, but hadn't I been doing the same to him? It was a classic case of two wrongs don't make a right. Now we'd found ourselves at a crossroads.

"I had to know for sure, so I sought you out."

"You stalked me," I correct him.

"Fine, I stalked you, Duchess. You're incredibly stalk-able."

I choose to take that as a compliment.

"Then at some point it stopped being about looking for answers and it just became about spending time with you," he confesses.

As hard as I try to hold on to my anger I feel it slipping slowly away from me. It leaks from my blood until I feel nothing but exhaustion. Jameson waits, his eyebrows furrowed, as I stay silent.

"I get it," I say finally.

"Because you were doing the same to me?" he asks.

"Maybe," I hedge. What's the fun in showing all my cards at once? Except I know he's already seen them. He's seen right through me. I won't be getting any tricks past him. The good news is, he won't be getting any past me either.

"So where do we go from here?"

"I don't care," he murmurs. This time I let him take my hand. "As long as we go there together."

"I don't think they make co-ed prison cells," I say flatly.

"Touché, Duchess."

"Please tell me you have a really, really good lawyer." We can't keep avoiding this, or avoiding the practical discussions that need to happen. "Speaking of which, do I need a really, really good lawyer?"

"Believe me, Detective Mackey is not interested in you," he says. "She had a few words with me for dragging you into this. I think she's convinced I paid you to say we were together that night."

Despite the conflicting emotions swirling inside of me I take offense at this. Maneuvering myself in the seat, I straddle him and wrap my arms behind his neck. "Did she honestly suggest my boyfriend needs to pay someone off to spend the night with him?"

He smirks, allowing a glimpse of the arrogant boy I'd met that night in his father's study. His hands circle my waist and press flat against the small of my back, drawing me closer to him.

My heart begins to pound along with a few other parts of me as our bodies press together, and without thinking I begin to rock against his groin seeking relief. "Maybe we should go inside, Duchess," he suggests, sweeping his lips lightly over my own.

"Too far," I whimper as I push the ache at my center against the rock hard bulge between my legs. His hands slide under my tank top to trail down my bare back.

"Tell me what you want," he groans, as I continue to rub myself against him.

"You."

"What about your checklist?"

"Fuck my checklist," I whisper into his ear, nipping it with my teeth.

"You're making it very hard to think clearly, Duchess."

"Then don't think," I urge him. "I just want to be someone else tonight," I say, recalling the words I spoke to him when we met.

"Carefree?" he offers, and I nod. "Believe me," he mutters with a frustrated groan, "I want nothing more than to strip you down and give you exactly what you're asking for, but I think that plan benefits from adding a bed to it."

"But the bed is so far," I moan, "and it's raining."

"And we're parked outside one of the busiest resorts in Las Vegas," he reminds me. But even as he speaks his hands tangle in my hair, drawing my lips to his once more. His body begins to move in unison with mine, meeting each push and grind of my hips with a thrust of his own. The denim of my jeans rasps against the sensitive spot begging for attention, and I begin to whimper.

"That's it, Duchess," he coaxes, his hands guiding my hips to move faster. "This is only a taste."

My muscles tense and I dig my fingernails into the back of his neck just as a rap at the window startles us apart.

"Um, Mister West?" The valet looks politely away

as he calls through the window. "Can we park your car for you?"

I look around and I'm embarrassed to see a number of hotel guests clustered around the entrance, phones in hand.

"Yes," Jameson calls back. The valet opens the driver door and offers me a hand to help me extricate myself from my precarious situation. As soon as I'm around the car I take a bow, careful to make sure my middle finger is hidden in plain sight. Enjoy the photos.

"That's enough, Duchess." Jameson puts a hand on the small of my back. He keeps it there as we make a dash for the entrance, and under its comforting warmth, I don't even notice the rain.

19

NO one's prepared for rain in the desert. We're half-drowned by the time we're inside the lobby. Jameson catches me around the waist, and spins me behind a column.

"Let's finish the game we started the night we met," he suggests, nuzzling along my jawline. He trails upward, until his lips find my earlobe, but he doesn't kiss me. Instead, he catches the tender shell between his teeth. The nip is playful, but the ache that elicits inside me is very serious.

"Truth or dare," I moan, not caring that half of Vegas could be Snapchatting us right now.

"Truth," he murmurs. The heat of his breath whispers unspoken promises, but it can't distract me from the question I need answered.

"Why did you come looking for me that day in the graveyard?" I ask.

"That's what you want to know?" He seems surprised, but he doesn't pull away from me. Instead, he moves his mouth back up to my ear. "There are three reasons, Duchess. Two I will share, but the other, I'm keeping in my pocket."

Does he feel the need to keep me guessing, too? It's a twisted game we're caught in, neither of us sure what the other's intentions are, and it's made all the more dangerous, because we've put our hearts at stake. "I'll settle for two," I breathe.

"Because I wanted to see you," he admits. It's not the answer I expect. That day, of all days, he should have had more important things on his mind, but as his hands grip my hips, I push the troubling thought down where it can't distract me.

"You want a better explanation," he guesses. He pulls away, only far enough so that our eyes can meet. "I didn't plan to leave you there that night. I didn't plan any of this, and I suppose I wanted you to know that."

"And the other reason?"

"I wanted to convince myself you did it, but instead I think I fell for you."

"How did you know I was there? Did you follow me?"

"I went to your house," he says, "And then I saw you running. So yes, Emma, I did follow you. Does that upset you?"

I swallow and nod. I can't admit that his explanation is reasonable, because if whatever's happening between us is going to work, there has to be some boundaries. "I need to know I'm still my own person and that you respect that."

Given how it hurts when he steps away from me, I need to remind myself of that, too.

"I'm sorry." Sincerity shines in his silver-blue eyes. "I suppose now isn't the time to bring up the security detail I'd like to place on you."

I raise one eyebrow, sliding my palms up his chest, and then I push him away. "I'm starting to think everyone's right, and you are crazy."

"Does that make you insane by association?" he asks.

"Maybe." I close my eyes and let out an annoyed huff of air.

"You have a terrible habit of ruining perfectly good dates."

"So this is finally a date." His mouth twists into a haughty grin that screams I told you so.

"Don't look so self-congratulatory," I warn him, "Not when I just told you that you're a first-class date wrecker."

He reaches out and fiddles with the hem of my tank. "But you have to understand, I was told those weren't dates."

"So you weren't trying?"

"Oh, I've been trying since the minute I met you, Duchess. It's just nice to know that I might be succeeding." His knuckles graze against my stomach as he continues to play with my shirt. Even the hint of his touch blazes a trail of fire in its wake. I know two things, then. Jameson West can take me when he wants me, and two, I'm totally screwed.

"Come on." He urges me away from the pillar. It's strange to think about going back upstairs. The place where our relationship began is almost where it ended. There's no security guard waiting at the private elevator, and I flash a concerned look at him.

"So you want to put a security detail on me, but no one's watching the gates to the kingdom?"

"Don't worry, Duchess," he says as he presses the elevator button. "I've had four times as many security cameras installed in the last week. You can't blink here without security knowing about it."

"But why not have the extra muscle?"

He laughs at this. "For someone who looked very resistant to the idea of having a body guard, you seem awfully concerned about my safety."

"I can't stand the idea of someone doing you bodily harm." I run my fingers across the flat plane of his abdomen. Of the two of us, he's in much more danger than I am. At least that's what I want to tell myself, even as I ignore the real danger I face. How I feel about Jameson is morphing and evolving so rapidly that it's hard to wrap my head around, but the very fact that I've never felt this way about anyone before tells me all I need to know. Yes, I am in danger of losing my heart to him.

"Then you understand how I feel," he says huskily.

At least if I do lose my heart to him, I'll be getting one in return.

"Your turn," he prompts, as the elevator light signals its imminent arrival.

I look him squarely in the eyes as the doors slide open behind us. "Dare."

"God, I was hoping you'd say that, Duchess." His hand fists in my shirt, dragging me inside the compartment. "This elevator only goes up," he reminds me. "So the only button I need to worry about pushing is yours. But," he backs me into the mirrored wall, his hips pressing roughly against mine. "If I hit this button, we'll have two minutes alone in here before security responds."

I follow his gaze to the panel, where a stop button is located next to one marked panic. "So what's your dare, then?" I ask him.

"If I hit that button, you have to accept it." He shifts his groin harder against mine, so that I can feel the long, hard outline of his dick.

I want more than two minutes with that, but I'll take what I can get. "I said dare, didn't I? Wait, are there cameras in here?"

The wicked grin that splits his face is answer enough. "But doesn't that make it better?"

"Dare," I repeat.

He presses the button. The elevator screeches to a halt as his lips cover mine.

"I dare you to hold out" he breathes against them. I lose that dare on the spot.

"You only have two minutes," I taunt.

"With two minutes, I could get you there twice, but I think I'll take my time." I get the sense that isn't a boast, but my heart sinks a little at the thought of having to wait. I have absolutely no intention of holding out on this one. Our mouths crush together as he slants his head, deepening the kiss, allowing his tongue to capture my own. When we break apart a few seconds later, we're breathless, but I shake my head.

"You're a good kisser, but you're not that good, West."

"I think you want to lose, Duchess. Now I'm going to make you wait even longer." He bends his head, denying me his kiss, but only so that he can start the slow progress from my collarbone to the valley between my breasts. My eyes clamp shut, as my head falls back, knocking against the mirror. When I feel the heat of his mouth settling over the peaks, I open one eye, and watch as he slowly begins to suck it through the fabric of my tank and bra.

Seeing it is almost as amazing as actually feeling it. It might not be enough to get me there, but I'm not going to complain. After a few seconds, he switches to the other side, repeating the move until I've begun to whimper. Then he releases me, and it takes all my willpower not to grab his hair and shove him back where he belongs.

Jameson straightens up, and traces a finger along the bow of my upper lip. "I could get you off that way," he promises, "but I'm feeling very selfish tonight." His finger runs along my lower lip, down my chin, and neck, forging a line down, down, down, until his hand reaches the waistband of my jeans. With one practiced move, he unbuttons them.

"Pink panties," he says with approval. "God, you're going to kill me, Duchess."

In fact, I am going to kill him, if he doesn't finish what he started soon. I buck against the hand still gripping my jeans. He takes the hint, and his hand flattens against my lower belly. He slides it past the thin satin of my panties, stopping just before he reaches the promised land.

"Look at me," he commands. "Show me your green eyes, Duchess."

I bite my lip as I open my eyes, trying to stay still.

"Still determined to win?" His finger slips to the precise point of my desire and begins to rub slow circles around it.

I nod, but my breath hitches in my throat.

"Don't pass out," he warns me quickening the pace. He crushes his body against mine, trapping his hand in place. His hips begin to imitate the rhythm, adding an insurmountable amount of pressure. "Show me how pretty you look when I'm giving you what you need, Duchess."

The breath I've been holding releases in a throaty

cry as I crack apart at the seams. My muscles spasm and I crumble into him. His mouth finds mine and he sucks his own pleasure from my lips. I have to press my thighs tightly together when he doesn't stop. Jameson takes the hint and withdraws his hand. He grabs my hip and kneads it as I come down from the amazing high of his touch.

"What happens when you lose a dare?" he asks.

I stare dreamily at him and smile. "I think you win the game."

20

MY legs shake as Jameson hits the button to restart the elevator. Best two minutes of my life. Judging from the pleased smirk on his face, he's happy about it, too. But when the elevator deposits us onto his private floor, we're greeted by the loud beat of bass. Jameson grabs my hand and drags me out, cursing under his breath. Given the shattering experience I just had, it takes more than a little effort to keep up with him, especially in heels.

"I cannot fucking believe this," he mutters as he leads me into the entertainment suite. It looks like a scene from last weekend: classmates passed out on the furniture, girls doing body shots on the bar, even Hugo waves from the couch.

Jameson turns to me. "I'm so sorry about this. Can you give me a minute?"

I nod but he's already abandoned me. I stand

awkwardly in the midst of my drunk schoolmates. So much for the romantic evening of bliss I've been promised. This is like a bad Vietnam flashback.

"Pawn star!" Hugo calls to me. "Did you miss me?"

"Like I missed the stomach flu," I respond with a grimace.

Hugo ditches the girl hanging off of him and wanders closer. "I see you traded up but I suppose damaged goods can be bought at a reduced price."

"I'd advise you to shut the fuck up before Jameson hears you." I'm through with his insults.

His mocking attitude evaporates and he takes a menacing step closer. "You have to do more than screw yourself into this crowd. I thought you figured that out when I left you there after that night, but since you didn't let me make it clear. You don't get to speak to us like that."

"Why, because the Housers always win?" I ask.

"Because you're trash."

"Sticks and stones Hugo," I say with a sigh. "If you'll excuse me I feel the need to throw up now." I turn on my heel and walk away my hands balling into fists at my side. If today has taught me anything is that's violence isn't the answer, even if it would be very satisfying.

"He's going to see through you," Hugo calls after me. "Just like Jonas. Just like the rest of us."

I refuse to turn around and acknowledge the last

comment even as it sticks in my back. Knowing something isn't true on a rational level doesn't always make it hurt less. I escort myself back to the entrance. The last time I walked around here unchaperoned bad things happened, but I'm not about to stand there and let Hugo hurl abuse at me. Crossing my arms over my chest I lean against the marble wall and wait for Jameson to return. After a few minutes I send him a text but I get no response.

I'm just about to head back into the chaos when the elevator slides open. Detective Mackey strides out, zeroing in on me. "Ms. Southerly."

I force a smile that's not fooling anyone.

"Are you here with Jameson West?" she asks.

I'm not sure how to answer that but it's not like I can hide the truth. "Yes."

"It sounds like there are quite a few people here with Jameson West." She cocks her head as if she's listening to the music. "We just got here," I rush to explain. It can't look good to be having a party on the one week anniversary of murder but I can tell from the calculated look on her face that she's not interested in my excuses.

"Where can we find him?" she asks me.

"What do you want with him?" I make a mental note to get the name of Jameson's lawyer and put it on my speed dial.

She pulls an envelope from her bag. "It's private business."

"I think he's with his sister," I say finally, "or at least he's looking for her."

"So then this is Monroe's idea of grieving?" Mackey guesses.

For no explicable reason I find myself growing defensive. "She's had a bit of a rough week."

"Emma." Mackey leans forward and lowers her voice to a conspiratorial whisper. "Don't try to excuse their behavior. Stay above it."

Is that what she thinks of me, that I'm above all of this? Jameson must have been right when he said she didn't suspect me but the fact does nothing to soothe me. The only way I can stay above this is with Jameson by my side doing the same, but he's not here.

"Excuse us," she waves on the officer waiting behind her. "We need to find your boyfriend."

I guess news travels fast. Then again with any luck the beginnings of our first sex tape have already made it onto YouTube. I slam my fist against the wall, remembering too late that it's marble. Clutching it, I groan. Then I hurry after her. Whatever Jameson has to face tonight, he won't do it alone. I catch up with her just as she finds him arguing with Monroe.

"Excuse me, Mr. West. Perhaps we can speak somewhere privately," Detective Mackey interrupts. Both Wests fall silent immediately and stare at her.

Jameson's eyes dart to mine over her shoulder. "Take care of her?" he asks me, glancing toward Monroe.

"You did not just ask her to do that!" Monroe stomps into the other room either oblivious to the fact that her brother is probably going to be arrested or indifferent to it. Despite his request I follow behind them as he leads them into a hall away from the crowd.

"Jameson West, I'm here to arrest you for assault."

"Is that what we're calling it?" he asks in confusion. "That's a majorly reduced charge."

"We received report of the assault," she continues ignoring his interjection, "this evening."

"Wait," he stops her, "who's claiming I assaulted them?"

"Jake Southerly."

I gasp and heads swivel in my direction but Jameson's eyes warn me to stay silent.

"Did you miss me that much, Detective? We both know these charges won't stick."

"Be that as it may we have a nice jail cell waiting for you." She turns to the officer behind her and nods. He walks forward cuffs in hand and begins to read Jameson his Miranda rights.

"Please find Monroe," Jameson calls ignoring him completely. "Check on her, then take her phone and call my mom."

I want to defend him and tell Detective Mackey that Jameson was protecting me but from the look in his eyes I know he doesn't want me to do that. It takes everything I can muster to keep my mouth shut.

"Some date," he says to me as they haul him toward the elevator.

"Maybe next time we could just grab some dinner," I suggest. Before they can stop me I run over and kiss him full on the lips. The officer leading him out breaks us apart.

"That's quite enough!" Detective Mackey warns us. She studies me curiously as we all stand there and wait for the elevator to arrive. When it does, she lets the officer take Jameson inside.

"Just a moment," she tells him. Then she turns to me. "What does he have on you?"

"Nothing." I hate her for even suggesting that I can be bought.

"I thought you were a smarter girl than that." She leaves the proclamation hanging in the air before she disappears into the elevator.

The doors shut and I stand there listening to the throb of music coming from the other room.

"You couldn't have broken up the party while you were at it," I say to the elevator doors. Then I steel myself and head back inside.

Monroe is nowhere to be found. I navigate through the crowd, careful to avoid Hugo. Coming around the corner to the kitchen where I cooked for Jameson, I halt as two voices rise angrily. Tiptoeing to the wall I get as close as possible, trying to listen in without being seen.

"You have no idea what you saw!"

I peek around the corner and find Monroe and Leighton in a face off. Given Leighton's knock-off of the Wicked Bitch's wardrobe, right down to the mournful black from head to toe. Is imitation still the sincerest form of flattery?

"I would never say anything," Leighton starts.

"No, it's about how you're mistaken because you couldn't possibly have seen that."

"But I did," Leighton says.

God does the girl have any sense of self-preservation about her? Even from here I can see the anger practically vibrating off of Monroe. "I saw him that night with him. I saw what he did to him, and I just want you to know ..."

"No," Monroe cuts her off. "You saw nothing and if you can't remember that, then remember this: without me you're nothing. I can destroy you just as fast as I made you."

I flatten against the wall as Monroe turns and stalks back to the party. Leighton stands there for a moment before she does the same.

What the hell was that about? What had Leighton seen? Why was Monroe so intent on keeping her quiet?

The fragile strands of trust binding my heart to Jameson's begin to fray. There's only one thing that Leighton could have seen that would scare Monroe this badly, but if she did why hasn't she said anything? But I already know the answer. Because she's scared of what will happen to her. Earlier I decided that I trusted Jameson. Now I have to face the possibility that despite that, he still might not be innocent. He told me himself he was drinking. If he lost his temper, could I blame him for what had happened? Would it change how I felt about him?

I want to believe it couldn't but as the pit in my stomach grows, I force myself to face the fact that it might. Rushing back into the other room, I search for Leighton. I finally find her near the bar doing tequila shots. I suppose blacking out might be preferable to remembering tonight. She spots me and shakes her head dropping the lime she's sucking on to the counter.

"You should go," she suggests. "If Monroe sees you here she is going to lose her mind."

"Believe me she already knows I'm here." Grabbing Leighton by her thin wrist, I tuck her away from the cluster of people at the bar and over near the windows overlooking the patio. People brush past us and the noise offers us cover. "I overhead you talking to Monroe."

She pales and glances nervously around us. Meanwhile, I keep my back to the crowd. Hopefully if Monroe is circling, she won't spot us. "I don't really care what anyone here thinks of me but I do care what they're saying about my boyfriend."

"Your boyfriend?" she says in confusion. "Look, obviously I didn't see what I thought I saw."

I want to yank her bleached blonde locks at the

root and shake her until she breaks like a piñata. "I heard you," I repeat. "I just need to know what you saw."

"Monroe was right," she says in a hurry. "It probably wasn't what I thought. I mean why would Jonas …"

"Jonas?" I cut her off. "I thought we were talking about Jameson."

She blinks rapidly before she giggles. "Jameson? Why would I be talking about him?"

"Maybe because he just got arrested," I say.

"The Wests have more money than God." She rolls her eyes and flips her hair over her shoulder like she's auditioning for a Barbie commercial. "He'll be playing golf faster than O.J."

"O.J. sat in prison for nearly two years," I tell her. "So try again. What were you talking to Monroe about?"

"It has nothing to do with Jameson," she repeats. "I know he didn't kill his father, because…"

She breaks off smiling widely at someone over my shoulder. It's the last thing I see before I'm thrown forward. My mind tries to put together the pieces as I slam into her. A hand. My back. Glass shattering as we crash through it. I don't have time to think as we fall the few feet onto the concrete.

I've never put much stock in mistakes. Despite the last year of my life, I didn't want my past choices to define me. Now I know I'm doomed to pay for every decision I've made. This is the realization that crashes into me as I fight to stay awake.

Red coats the back of my eyelids as I drift between the real world and the dark. Lights flash, blinding me momentarily as I blink into the rain. It takes a moment for her to come into focus, but when she does everything about her is wrong. Her arms and legs are twisted in unnatural directions like a broken doll. Glass digs into my hands as I claw across the wet pavement toward her. My palm slips as it hits a warm and slippery substance pooling around her head. Her lips are turning blue, but there's a smile fixed on her face as her eyes stare into the starless midnight sky. She looks happy as if she's about to greet a friend.

I say her name, I shake her, and then, I scream. And scream. And scream.

ACKNOWLEDGMENTS

Very few people knew about this super secret project until it was finished, so I have to give them major props for being patient with me as I figured out all the twists and turns.

First off, I could not survive without my partner in crime, sister, and business manager, Elise Lee. Copper boom!

Rebecca Yarros, you are the best cheerleader and soul sister that I can imagine. S.L. Scott, your enthusiasm is limitless and I always walk away from my conversations feeling inspired. Shayla, I'm not going to butcher your last name, but thank you for all the late night talks and writing sprints. I'm so blessed to have you all in my life.

Louise Fury, your name suits you. I pinch myself whenever I tell someone I am your client. Thank you for your support and guidance. This is the beginning of a beautiful relationship.

Becca Mysoor, you walked into my world with fabulous lipstick and I knew we would be friends. You are the sweetest lipstick guru I know and one hell of an editor. Thank you for taking a chance on me.

To the authors who inspire me every single day to keep writing and telling stories by being the genuine article. Thank you, Meredith Wild for raising the bar and limo rides. Audrey Carlan, your beautiful spirit encourages me every day. There are so many others I could name here but it would take another book. I am beyond privileged to be part of this industry with you.

Jackie, thank you for being the glue I need when I'm on deadline.

To the entire Ivy Estate team, you're making my dreams come true.

To the Loves, I don't know where to begin. You make me want to write every single day. Thank you for letting me tell you stories.

No book would have a life without its readers. Thank YOU for reading this book. You're the reason I do this.

And to Josh, I'm so glad that we can talk or not talk all day long. You make me believe in true love.

www.ingramcontent.com/pod-product-compliance
Lightning Source LLC
Chambersburg PA
CBHW010435170726
48283CB00011B/3223